BLUSHING BIRDIE

GEORGIA PEACHES, BOOK 1

VANESSA GRAY BARTAL

DRY CREEK PRESS

"*H*ave you ever realized time is running out for you to turn into the person you know you're supposed to be?"

The question was posed to Birdie as she sat behind her desk at the travel agency. No one under the age of fifty used travel agents anymore. Her job was slowly dying, but Birdie didn't mind. She had two others to supplement her meager income and she figured by the time her career was really over, she would have found something else to replace it. And she loved her elderly customers. Occasionally one of them lived up to the stereotype of being a curmudgeon, but for the most part they were personable and sweet. Often when they were in her chair, it was part of a long-held dream, something they had been saving toward for years, possibly even decades.

"How so?" Birdie asked, resting her elbows on the desk as she leaned forward. For some reason her heart was beating hard, as if she were about to hear life changing information.

Mrs. Miller pushed up her glasses and also leaned forward, her papery voice infusing with passion. "Everyone has a version of themselves they think they are. So often it's not the reality. We often think when we grow up we're going to be more than what we are. I'm running out of time to be the person I think I am. I've been waiting for some unknown thing, some catalyst that would be the spark telling me it's time to start living my life, but I'm done waiting." She plunked her purse on the desk. "I want to go to Italy."

Birdie blinked at her, dazed. There was no reason for the foggy feeling now washing over her brain. She had planned more than a dozen successful trips to Italy. Despite never having been, she knew it inside and out, knew all the best hotels, the highlights, things to see and do, places to eat, churches and museums to visit. But on this day, at this moment, her brain blanked. All she could focus on were the first words Mrs. Miller said. *Have you ever realized time is running out for you to turn into the person you know you're supposed to be?* It was the exact thing Birdie didn't know she had secretly been thinking, and the thought lanced her soul, slicing through layers of denial, of walls and fortresses she didn't know she'd built.

Her mind zoomed back into focus and she realized Mrs. Miller was staring at her, waiting on a reply to her dramatic statement.

"Italy is lovely this time of year. Where do you want to go?" Birdie asked, her mouth dry, her throat parched. She took a surreptitious sip of the now cold tea in her travel mug.

Mrs. Miller rooted in her oversized purse and deposited a notebook on the table. "Everywhere, but it will have to be on a budget. I sketched out a possible itinerary. But I need help with the logistics."

"Logistics are my specialty," Birdie said. She meant it to be a light-hearted statement, but the disquiet now fogging her mind made the words fall flat. Mrs. Miller blinked at her then brushed the words aside, too intent on her own agenda to be worried by Birdie's apparent mental breakdown.

With effort, Birdie pulled her mind back to work, reached for Mrs. Miller's itinerary, and started a new file on her computer, the familiar clacking of her keyboard working to push away the last of the unsettling feelings.

In no time they had created a formal outline for Mrs. Miller's trip. "I'll work on this until we meet again next week. In the meantime, I want you to make certain this is what you want. Once the deposits are paid, there's no going back," Birdie warned.

Mrs. Miller gave one, curt nod. "Exactly," she agreed. She pushed up her glasses, gathered her purse, thanked Birdie, and left.

Birdie sat staring at her computer, trying hard to focus on Mrs. Miller's itinerary and not the words that felt like they were worming into her brain. *...time is running out for you to be the person you know you're supposed to be.* The harder she tried to push the phrase away, the more it echoed through her mind.

When she could take it no more, she scooted away from her desk, stood, and walked out the door. It was a bit early for a break, but her boss wouldn't mind. No customers were scheduled for the rest of the day, and it wasn't the sort of place that had a lot of walk-ins.

Birdie stretched, pulling at tense muscles. They hadn't been tight until the disconcerting conversation with Mrs. Miller. Since then she felt as if she had been holding everything in, clenching everything to keep herself in check.

Walk to the door and go outside, she commanded herself, hoping that if she kept giving her body simple directions it would comply instead of pondering as her brain currently wanted.

"Be back in a minute," Birdie called. Her boss was in the back, heating a cup of coffee. "Do you want anything?"

"I'm good," Shelley called.

The next sound was the tinkling of the bell over the door as Birdie let herself out. She paused on the sidewalk, taking a deep breath. Was it an attempt to relax or to fortify herself?

When she passed the storefront next to the travel agency, she thought it was the latter. *Don't look, don't look, don't look,* she coached herself. She hardly ever looked. Only a couple of times had she glanced inside and caught him looking at her. *Him.* The enemy.

But today her body complied with directions, her neck refusing to swivel, her eyes not daring to peer in the glass door. Head up, she marched past the storefront as if she were on a mission.

Good job, she cajoled, allowing herself to feel some small measure of satisfaction. She hadn't glanced at the enemy, hadn't given him the satisfaction.

The next doorway she reached, she not only looked inside, she grabbed the door and gave it a hard tug. Plastering a smile on her face, she stepped cheerfully inside.

"What's wrong?" her brother greeted her from his spot behind the counter.

Birdie's smile fled. Blast him and his prescient knowledge of her moods. "Nothing," she lied, conjuring another smile, one she hoped was more convincing. It wasn't that she was above confiding in her big brother, merely that she had no idea what the problem was. Something had been disquieted in her soul. Why, she had no idea. Until she figured that out, she didn't want to talk about it with anyone, not even her closest relative/best friend. "Just stretching my legs. Got anything new in today?"

His head nudged toward the new release section before his eyes lowered to whatever he'd been doing before she arrived. Birdie wandered over to the area he'd indicated and began picking up the new arrivals. Her brother was living her dream as the owner of a bookshop, and she loved him too much to be envious. Instead she settled for living vicariously through him, showing up every day—sometimes more than once a day—to see what was new in his world.

She held the book to her nose and inhaled. *New book smell.* There was really nothing like it. The scent eased her in ways she couldn't describe, settling that little restless something deep within. Or at least it usually did. Today it didn't begin to subdue the tiny hole Mrs. Miller's words had torn open, the one that was barreling toward becoming a yawning chasm. Why had they bothered her so much, those words?

Because it's everything you've ever felt, but never put a name to.

She sank to the chair propped helpfully in the new book section. *Oh.* Birdie had always secretly thought she would someday be something more than she was, a better version of herself, stronger, braver, more adventurous, more put together. Instead she was a late bloomer who never bloomed.

As she sat and clutched the new book to her chest, her mind ran rampant with all the ways she had failed to improve. *Mousy. Boring. Inexperienced. Fearful. Settled. Ordinary. Unloved.* In high school she had found consolation by telling herself things would get better. After adolescence her life would come together in unimaginable ways. She would be fitter, prettier, more popular, universally desired, fulfilled, full of purpose. Instead she worked three dull jobs to make ends meet, still lived with her mother, and had exactly one friend—her brother.

"What's up, kiddo?" Sterling came over and sat cross-legged beside her on the floor. He had always been the more interesting sibling. Outgoing, charming, intelligent, and athletic, people liked him. Even his name was indicative of his nature. *Sterling. True, trustworthy, valuable.* And though he was only three years older, he had always treated her as a treasured little sister, never as an annoyance. In short, she idolized him.

"Do you ever want more than this life, Sterling?" Birdie asked.

He tilted his head at her. "Multiple lives? Past lives? Eternal life? Give me more clues, and I'll point you to the correct section for guidance."

"More *joie de vivre* in the life we're currently living," she explained.

Now his head tilted in the opposite direction. "What's up, Birdie?"

"I don't know," she said, sighing helplessly. "I thought I would be different by now, I guess."

"Different than what?" he asked.

"Than I used to be," she said.

"You've always been the same," he said.

"I know. That's the problem," she said.

"What's wrong with you? I happen to like you." Sterling was the type of guy who could say that to his sister and have it be normal and endearing, not a big deal, merely the way he was.

"You have to like me; you're my brother," she said.

"No, I have to tolerate you. I have to love you. No one says I have to like you, I just do," he said.

"I don't think I do," she said, her tone dismal.

Sterling stood and held out his hand to her. "Come on."

She didn't have to ask where. She put her hand trustingly in his and allowed him to pull her up, trotting dutifully behind as he wove her through the store. Sterling genuinely believed all of life's problems could be solved with a book. Birdie happened to believe the same, so it was with something like relief that she allowed him to lead her to the self-help section. "Here you go," he said. He deposited her with a flourish and squeezed her shoulders before returning to his station at the front of the store.

"What should I get?" she asked, her eyes darting frantically over the few dozen volumes before her.

"You'll know it when you see it, I bet," Sterling replied nonchalantly.

"You're taking my mental breakdown in great stride," she called.

"Rest assured I'm in tatters on the inside," he replied, picking up a price gun and continuing to mark the latest shipment of books.

Her eyes scanned the titles, feeling more than a bit ridiculous. *Mend over Matter, Fix Yourself First, Human, Heal Thyself!, Today is Your Day!,* and on and on they ran. She could almost hear her mother cringing at the thought of anyone using one of these books to try and become a better person. *She* was cringing. On the other hand…

Her fingers skimmed the titles, eyes closed. *Eeny, meanie, miney…*Her hand grasped a spine. She pried open her eyes to see what she had blindly selected. *Mend Over Matter.* Great. Not allowing herself to peek inside to see what insipid nonsense might be in store, she trudged to the front of the store and laid her selection on the counter.

Sterling's brow arched, but he didn't say a word as he rang her up. In a perfect world, a brother wouldn't charge a sister for buying his wares. In reality Sterling needed every penny to keep afloat, and Birdie would have insisted on paying anyway. It was something they settled a long time ago when he first opened the shop. Most of the books she wanted she checked out from the library for free. But not this. She imagined trying to sneak this title through the checkout at the library, and her cheeks flamed. Bad enough to share her humiliation with her brother.

"You want a bag?" Sterling asked.

Birdie nodded, cheeks still a healthy shade of pink.

He slid the book into a plain, brown paper bag, and she breathed a sigh of relief. "Thanks."

"Birdie, you okay?" Sterling tried one more time, his tone solemn and worried, the consummate big brother.

She nodded because of course she was, wasn't she? This, whatever it was, had to be a blip. There was no way one small sentence from a stranger could throw her world into such turmoil.

If she'd known how wrong she would be about that, she would have slipped the book back on the shelf and run out the door.

CHAPTER 3

irdie's mind was distracted as she headed back to her office, too much to discipline her eyes where they were supposed to go. Her head swiveled, glancing in the glass door of the repair shop. He was there, of course, her enemy. His eyes followed her, tracking her movement from one side of the shop to the other like those black plastic cat clocks, the ones where the eyes and tail swish back and forth. His head remained firmly in place, but those eyes watched her, as they always did when she failed to keep herself in check. Too late she forced her face to the front, ignoring him once again.

"How was Sterling?" Shelley greeted her with the tone, the one women reserved for Sterling. In young women it was always a dreamy sort of hopefulness, making his name almost a sigh, followed by a little pause. *Sterling...* In older women, women like Shelley, it was said with a maternal sort of pride, as if they'd had some hand in the wonderful way he turned out. Birdie was certain no one had ever said her name with any sort of inflection, either good or bad. She was always just *there,* hovering in the background unseen, the unnoticed comma in a run on sentence.

"Grand," Birdie said with the same note of pride. She had never been jealous of her brother and his much beloved nature, not one minute of their lives. Instead she had indulged in delight by association. She might not have much else going for her, but she had always been Sterling Thompson's favorite (and only) little sister.

"Such a good boy," Shelley muttered. She reached for her coffee, the one she had heated as Birdie was leaving. It was her routine to nurse the singular cup of coffee all day long. She prepped it on arrival in the morning and then forgot about it so often during the day that by the time closing rolled around, it had turned into a dark and bitter sludge. Most days she grimaced and dumped it down the sink untasted. Now as soon as her hand came in contact with the cool mug, she frowned and stood to go to the microwave in the back for another turn at warming the already inedible brew.

Birdie glanced up with her own frown. Something was different, but what? "Hey, Shelley, the clock's broken."

Shelley returned, her frown deepening to a scowl as she stared at the clock. It was an heirloom, a hand me down from her grandparents. "Oh, no." She checked her watch, comparing it with the nonmoving time on the wall. "I'm going to have to get it fixed, but I have a client coming in a few minutes." She glanced hopefully at Birdie. "Could you...?" the request trailed off unspoken. Shelley wasn't the type to assume too much, and Birdie wasn't her personal assistant. But they were friends. At any other time Birdie would have jumped in and volunteered to take the clock. But her stomach twisted at the thought. Still, though, they were friends, and Shelley was a good boss.

"I'll run it next door," Birdie volunteered. If Shelley heard the reluctance in her tone, she didn't call it out.

"Thank you so much," Shelley said, sounding relieved. She settled at her desk, the coffee once again forgotten. Birdie considered reminding her, but she would discover it as soon as her clients left and she heated soup for a post-lunch snack.

Birdie turned her attention to the clock, standing on her toes to remove it from the wall. It was heavier than it looked. She stumbled slightly under the weight of it, letting a portion of it dig into her shoulder for support.

"That looks bigger than I remember. Let me get the door," Shelley said, darting from behind the desk to open it.

"Thanks," Birdie said, panting slightly. She exited the travel agency and walked five steps, pausing outside the repair shop in consternation. Shelley's help hadn't extended to this door. She glanced inside, but no one was there. Sighing, she set down the clock and tried the handle. It turned. She propped the door with her foot, picked up the clock and made her way inside.

"Just a second," a voice called from somewhere in the back.

Birdie set down the clock, tilting it gently against the base of the counter.

The owner of the voice emerged a few seconds later and stopped short, staring wordlessly at Birdie who stared at him wordlessly in return. She had never seen him up close before, always hating him from a distance on principle. He was…quite cute, she realized with a disconcerting flutter of nerves. Her first instinct was to blurt things to fill the awkward silence. But it was his shop and he was the enemy so she said nothing.

He eyed her, waiting her out.

She eyed him in return, not daring to blink.

His gaze scanned her up and down, assessing. Birdie forced herself to stand still, to not react. She wasn't the sort of woman people studied, never had been. She was the woman easily skipped over, the human equivalent of background noise. When his eyes returned to hers, he patted his palms on the counter between them.

Stooping, Birdie picked up the clock and hefted it onto the counter. He turned it over, his eyes narrowing in concentration. After a few minutes inspection, he reached for a small business card and scrawled on the back of it, sliding it across the counter into Birdie's waiting fingers.

She pulled the card close to read it. *Hayden Paxton, Second Time Around Repairs.* Beside the block printed words, he had scrawled a date, a week away along with the word, "Pickup."

Birdie tucked the card into her palm and took a step back and then a few more until she reached the door. Hayden's unblinking gaze never waivered. Birdie groped blindly for the door behind her. At last her palm found purchase with the handle and turned it, easing through once it was opened. Now on the sidewalk, her eyes remained focused on Hayden until, at last, his focus returned to the clock in front of him. With a slight frown, he leaned closer, inspecting it, dismissing her as if he'd said the words.

When she returned to the office, Shelley was with her customers. Birdie slipped unobtrusively into place, clicked on Mrs. Miller's file, and forced herself to work, refusing to let her mind dwell even for a moment on the odd encounter with Hayden Paxton. It wasn't until much later that she remembered the spur-of-the-moment book she'd purchased at Sterling's store. What had she been thinking buying a self-help manual? And in front of her perfect big brother, no less.

She took it out of the bag as soon as she was home, inspecting the embarrassing cover. To be fair, there wasn't anything on the cover but words, but the words were embarrassing enough. *Mend Over Matter.* Could the title be anymore humiliating? Probably.

Absently, her fingers skimmed through the book until at last the first chapter was propped in front of her. Each chapter was titled with pithy little sayings. Chapter One was "The You You want To Be!" *What's a You You?* Birdie wondered. "Have you ever felt like you were missing out?" That was the first sentence and Birdie rolled her eyes. Could it be any more vague? Plus who didn't feel like they were missing out? Everyone felt left out sometimes. Frustrated, she returned to the book and continued to read.

Have you ever felt like your life was a movie, but instead of being the main star you're a passive sidekick?

Birdie stopped reading. That, in a nutshell, was her entire life. Sterling was the star, had always been the star, would always be the star. Birdie was the sidekick, and sometimes not even that. Much of the time she had been the extra standing in the background, trying to make it look as if she were fitting in the scene when, really, she felt a peevish combination of spectacle and invisible. She sometimes thought everyone must be able to sense how thoroughly she didn't fit in, but she was beginning to realize it was worse than that: no one was paying enough attention to care.

Frowning now, she tucked the book closer and read with a new sort of fervor. If this book could change the invisible nature of her existence, maybe it had the answers she was looking for, the certain something her life had been lacking.

You can't expect to be the star of the show if you don't know what the movie is. So before you go any further, what do you want, friend? What. Do. You. Want?

It was written exactly like that, with a period after each word, and Birdie gave each its due pause. What. Did. She. Want?

That was the problem; she had no idea.

CHAPTER 4

After two hours at home, it was time to go to her second job at the library. Their small town had a low cost of living, but it also had lousy pay and few job opportunities. Birdie had three jobs to make ends meet. She worked twenty hours at the travel agency, twenty at the library, and fifteen keeping books for various businesses. That was her degree, an associates in accounting. She could doubtless make more if she did it fulltime, but it wasn't where her heart lay.

Where is your heart? She heard the question in the same voice she read *Mend Over Matter*, as if a movie narrator was speaking. If her passion wasn't in numbers, where was it? That would have been a more useful question before she got a degree in something, but at twenty six, it wasn't too late to change direction. Was it?

The library was small and not often busy in the evenings. Birdie almost took the self-help book to read but thought better of it. Not only would she be mortified if someone caught her, but she wanted to read it slowly, to ponder each ridiculous sound bite for snippets of truth. As suspected, the place was empty. Birdie grabbed a knitting magazine and sat behind the desk.

Do I want to be the kind of person who spends her evening at the library reading a knitting magazine? She had the feeling she shouldn't want that, but she had no idea what she would want to do instead. She enjoyed knitting, and she loved the library, always had. It had been her childhood refuge and remained so as an adult. She had been thrilled when the opportunity to work there became available, giving her access to as many new books as Sterling's store.

She was halfway through the knitting magazine when a book landed on the counter in front of her. Usually Birdie heard someone enter and put away whatever she was working on in order to be available. The thump of the book on the counter startled her. She glanced up and for the second time that day found herself looking into the face of Hayden Paxton, fixit man, her sworn enemy. His gaze was as unwavering as it had been a few hours ago, and so was hers. She usually offered up a friendly greeting to anyone who entered, but opening her mouth now felt like losing. So she remained silent as she slid her magazine closed and reached for his library card.

She wasn't supposed to pretend to notice the things people checked out, but of course she did. And she made secret judgments accordingly. Hayden had selected a John le Carré novel, one late enough in the series to prove himself a real fan. Birdie studied the book, thinking. She was something of a book whisperer, in possession of the ability to choose books for people with scary accuracy. Based on his current selection, there was a book she knew he'd love. She grasped the book, chancing a glance at him. His eyebrows rose in question. Before she could think it through too much, she disappeared to the correct shelf, reached for the book she wanted, brought it back, and checked him out, sliding both books across the counter to him.

Hayden picked up the new book, read the back cover with serious eyes, then looked at Birdie, tipping his head in a little salute before disappearing outside. Birdie stared after him, her blinks returning slowly until her phone buzzed with a text from her brother.

Heading to the gym. Wanna go?

She smiled, preparing to send her standard answer of, *Can't, got to stay home and lobotomize myself,* when her hand paused. If she was trying for self-improvement, she might as well start on her body.

Though not fat by anyone's standards, she was rather soft all over, sort of like a thin pillow.

Sure. I have to change first. Meet you there.

She hit send and started a countdown, waiting for Sterling's speedy reply. He didn't disappoint. Almost as soon as she finished, he returned with,

Are you being held hostage? Is this a covert cry for help? Do you need to call 911 and order a pizza to confuse your captors?

Maybe I've developed a sudden and keen interest in physical fitness. Ever think of that?

No....Are you okay? For real?

She smiled at her phone. *I'm okay for real. Just in the mood for something new.*

This is definitely new. See you there.

Birdie tucked her phone in her pocket and began closing procedures for the library. Less than an hour later she was her brother's guest at his twenty four hour gym, and she felt unaccountably nervous.

"I don't know how to use any of these machines," she said.

"Why are you whispering?" Sterling asked. "You're not in the library anymore."

"I feel like they'll hear me and know."

"No one else is here," he said.

"I was talking about the machines. They seem judgy," she said. "That one has its arms out in a defensive manner."

"Stop anthropomorphizing the workout equipment," Sterling said. "If you can't figure something out, ask me. No one knows what they're doing the first time out."

She squinted up at him. "Have you ever once had to ask how to use any of this equipment?"

He shrugged one shoulder. "I was really young when I started."

Birdie suppressed a sigh. Of course Sterling hadn't asked for help and of course he wouldn't say so and risk hurting her feelings. Sometimes he was too good to be true, even for someone who had known him all her life. It wasn't as if Birdie was a total screwup, but even being mediocre felt inadequate in light of his virtuosity.

The door squeaked and both of them turned to the entrance. For a wild second, Birdie was sure it would be Hayden Paxton, as if perhaps they were on some kind of continuous path, like a Mobius strip, and destined to run into each other until one of them cracked and spoke. But of course it wasn't. It was Duncan, Sterling's best friend since childhood.

"The little sister," Duncan said, stepping forward and giving Birdie's shoulder a light shove.

"The best friend," she returned, shoving his shoulder in return.

"Never seen you in here before," he said, shoving her shoulder again.

"Didn't anyone ever tell you not to hit girls?" she asked, shoving both his shoulders.

"Just Sterling, but when have I ever listened to him?" Duncan said, poking her belly button, hard enough to make her smack his hand. Somehow she had inherited the brother/sister dynamic with Duncan instead of her actual brother. They had always bickered, for as long as she could remember. So long that she wasn't sure if she actually disliked him. Was she jealous of Sterling and Duncan's close friendship? Perhaps. All she had was Sterling and their mom and, in the most technical sense, their father.

"All right, you two," Sterling said mildly, his eyes and fingers on his phone as he sent and received a few texts. "Don't pester Birdie. She's here to learn."

"I've been waiting for this day. I have so much to teach her," Duncan said.

"I'm not here to learn about bad pickup lines and self aggrandizement," Birdie returned.

"Then why'd you come, Chickie?" Duncan said, using the nickname she hated. It was bad enough to be named after fowl. At least he could call her by the one that isn't routinely plucked and eaten.

"I'm writing a paper on men who stare at themselves and grunt while they work out. Is it okay if I quote you?" she asked.

He grinned and tugged on the hair she'd hastily tossed into a ponytail. "If that's your way of saying you missed me, I forgive you."

Birdie rolled her eyes and turned to Sterling. "Where should I start?"

"On the elliptical. It's easy on the joints but still a good workout," he said vaguely, his mind still on his phone.

Birdie wanted to ask who he was texting, but on the other hand she didn't want to know. If it was his girlfriend, she was afraid she wouldn't be able to cover her reaction. His girlfriend wasn't one of Birdie's favorite people. The less said about her, the better. Duncan caught her eye, and she wondered if he was thinking the same thing because he gave her a dissatisfied little frown and shook his head. He didn't like the girlfriend, either. It was the one thing they had in common. That and their possessive jealousy over Sterling.

Birdie stood on the elliptical and stared at the board, trying to figure out if there was some trick to making it work. There wasn't. It actually was as easy as Sterling had said it would be, and she felt silly for being so intimidated by it. Of course she still had no idea how to use any of the other fancy equipment, but at least she had conquered this one thing.

She swished for a while in silence while the men did whatever they were doing with weights. She had no idea what it was, but it seemed to require two of them. They worked seamlessly, as if they'd done it many times before. Birdie tamped down a small spark of envy over their camaraderie. She had never had a Duncan, no best friend who would be willing to show up at nine on a Thursday to help her lift weights. She had only ever had a Sterling, and she had to share him with Duncan.

As if he knew she was thinking of him, Duncan lifted his head and made eye contact in the mirror. Birdie stuck out her tongue at him. He meandered over and upped the difficulty on the elliptical with a muttered, "At least pretend to push yourself, wimp."

"Hate you," Birdie said, panting a little now.

"Tell me something I don't know," he said, hitting the button once more.

She struggled in agonized silence a while, wiping sweat with the back of her hand. Would she be able to use her legs tomorrow? Doubtful. Behind her the men were talking. She mostly tuned them out until Duncan perked up.

"Dude, guess who I saw yesterday."

"I will, but after we turn thirty, you're going to have to stop 'dude-ing' me," Sterling said, pressing the heavy weight away from his chest.

"Never. I'll dude you until we die. Anyway, I saw Paxton, strutting around town like he owns it. I hate that guy." He took Sterling's weight and racked it.

Birdie came to such a sudden halt she tripped and had to grab for the edge of the elliptical to right herself.

"Smooth, Grace," Duncan said.

Birdie didn't respond. She hopped off the machine, cleaned it, and meandered over to the men, making a show of inspecting the weights. Not content to leave her alone, Duncan picked up a ten-pound weight and gave it to her. She made a show of pretending to lift it, hoping he would continue his conversation. With a sigh, he curled her bicep, showing her the proper way to lift the weight.

"Paxton moved back about a month ago," Sterling said, straining against the much heavier weight in his hands. "He moved into his dad's shop."

"Right next door to yours? The nerve of that guy," Duncan said furiously.

"Why do you hate him?" Birdie asked.

Duncan's sharp-eyed gaze swiveled accusingly to her. "Because he's the enemy, Chick."

"Pipe down, General Patton. I'm not denying he is, I'm merely wondering why. Not sure I ever got the full story there."

Sterling sat up and wiped his sweaty hands on a towel. "You know how some people you have bad blood with for no apparent reason?"

"Not really, unless you count Dad," Birdie said. "And Duncan, obviously."

Duncan rolled his eyes, but he was smiling.

Sterling tossed her a sad little smile and gave her shoulder a sympathetic squeeze. "It was like that with me and Hayden Paxton. From my earliest memories, we never got along. We competed over everything—girls, school, sports."

"He was a total…" Duncan began before tossing Birdie a look and amending what he was originally going to say, "jerk. He had this cocky smile that was so punchable." As if to illustrate the point, his fist curled.

"Yeah, but it's not like you ever got in any actual fights, right?" Birdie said.

They looked at her like she was crazy. "Yeah, Birdie, a lot of them," Sterling said.

"You fought?" Birdie breathed. "Where was I?"

Sterling shrugged. "We didn't get caught. It was usually after hours, at parties and such. And then senior year…" he trailed off. This part Birdie remembered.

"He beat you for quarterback."

Sterling swallowed hard and nodded. "And got a football scholarship."

The one he hadn't gotten, the one he likely would have gotten if Hayden hadn't taken his place. The one he had desperately needed. The one that meant he ended up putting himself through community college, getting a lackluster degree that led to his current status— barely making ends meet as a bookseller in their tiny town.

"Oh," Birdie said.

"Yeah, oh," Duncan said, taking the opportunity to jump in with his opinion. He pointed his finger in Birdie's face. "So stay away from him."

She shoved his hand away and rolled her eyes. "Yes, Duncan, I'm such a guy magnet. There's a real danger of me attracting my brother's sworn enemy."

"You're not…" Duncan began, staring at her. He trailed off, flustered. "You're not so bad, Chick."

"Is that praise or desperation talking?" Birdie asked, poking him.

"Maybe a little of both," Duncan said, regaining his equilibrium.

"Just saying the older I get, the crazier women seem. At least you're not crazy."

"Give it time," Sterling said.

"Uh," Birdie said, hands on hips in an affronted manner. Sterling had never been one to tease.

"Seriously, Birdie, it runs in the family," he said, winding his finger around his ear.

"I am not Dad," Birdie objected.

Sterling muttered something under his breath as Duncan switched her dumbbell to the other hand. Birdie couldn't be sure, but it sounded like, "That makes one of us." But of course that couldn't be it. Her brother was the sanest person she knew. Wasn't he?

CHAPTER 5

"When's the last time you talked to your dad?"

Those were her mother's greeting words when Birdie stumbled from her bedroom the next morning in search of coffee. Birdie waited to answer until she'd taken her first sip. When discussing her father, it was always best to be fortified with caffeine.

"It's been a couple of weeks," Birdie said. "Why?"

Her mother similarly took her time before answering. "He left a couple messages on my voicemail last night."

"What time last night?" Birdie asked.

"Three AM."

The two women blinked at each other. Her parents were the two most polar opposite people on the planet. How they ever got together in the first place was beyond Birdie's understanding. She had spent an inordinate amount of time trying to picture them young and in love, before the reality of life intervened and made them into the people they were today.

Her mother was calm, stoic, reserved, so protective of herself she appeared cold to those on the outside who didn't realize what a big heart she guarded. When she was younger, Birdie had always seen her father as being merely emotional, the opposite of her mother. As she got older she realized it was something more. He was likely bipolar, though there was no official diagnosis because he eschewed medication and psychiatric care. All Birdie knew for certain was that his wild mood swings were exhausting and frightening, especially in comparison to her stolid mother. He had never been physically abusive to any of them, never raised his hand during one of his rage meltdowns, never even threatened such a thing. But Birdie was scared of him all the same because sometimes the emotional toll was as bad as the physical. He had left bruises all over her, but none of them were on the outside where people could see. Birdie had learned to hold herself away from her father as a self-protective measure. And he made it easy because he made no secret of his preference for Sterling.

"I'll call him," Birdie said, gripping her mug more tightly. The upside of her parents' divorce was that her mother was no longer subject to her father's moods. She had found some measure of freedom in the intervening years, and she reveled in it. The downside was that Sterling and Birdie would never be free of their father, and now they lacked their mother as a protective buffer. His care and oversight now fell solely to them. Birdie had never felt more lacking than she did in her ability to rightly care for her father. Sterling shouldered much of the weight for keeping him from sinking too far on one of his lows or attempting to keep him reined in during one of his highs. So far he hadn't done anything too outlandish. It could be worse, she knew that. But just because it wasn't as bad as it could be didn't mean it was good.

"He likely won't answer," her mother said.

Birdie took another sip of coffee, eyes closed. "I'll stop over before work."

Her mother squeezed her shoulder without comment. Birdie hurried through her morning routine. She would have to rush to stop by her dad's and make it to work on time. She scurried to her car and tried to tamp down the encroaching anxiety going to her father's house always evoked. Theirs had never been an easy relationship. Her dad saw Birdie as a miniature of her mother—closed off, standoffish, unemotional. Birdie resented his inability to understand both her and her mom. How did he not realize that they were both merely self-protective? That, to anyone safe, they were warm and caring? The problem was that her father wasn't safe. His love felt too insubstantial, as if the onus for his approval was based on her accomplishments. He had always loved Sterling, always taken pride in his sports accolades. Though a strong student, Birdie had never had those sorts of proofs of her abilities, at least not the kind he cared about, the kind he could revel in. While he had never said anything outright mean to Birdie, neither had he said anything loving. Birdie vacillated between wanting his approval and wanting to avoid him for self-preservation.

She arrived on his doorstep and knocked, wondering if other daughters let themselves in without warning, wondering if other daughters felt certain of their welcome.

After a few repeated knocks her father stumbled to the door bleary eyed. "Birdie," he said, blinking owlishly at her.

Her name seemed to be the one connection between them. She was named after his beloved grandmother. Birdie wasn't certain if the reminder was pleasant because of the association or a disappointment because she fell so short of his expectations.

"How's it going, Dad?" she asked.

"Fine," he said, still not bothering to invite her inside.

"Mom said you left her some messages," she said.

His eyes narrowed at the mention of her mother. He was the one who sought a divorce, and he was the one who was still angry about it. Birdie thought it was likely she would never understand him. "I was thinking about things," he said.

"What kind of things?" Birdie asked.

He sighed, his shoulders slumping. "Life. There's a sick little girl in Kansas."

To an outsider, it might seem like a non sequiter, but Birdie understood. On the day of her high school graduation he had shown up hollow eyed, gutted by the plight of a war torn tribe of African children. It was all he had talked about the entire day. Not once did he offer Birdie his congratulations or say he was proud of her. He hadn't given her a gift, but he *had* donated a hundred dollars to the charity that oversaw the African children. It was one of the many perplexing discrepancies in his nature—a massive heart for hurting people far away and complete disregard for the pain of his daughter.

"A sick little girl in Kansas," Birdie prompted.

"She needs a new medicine but Congress won't approve the drug," he continued, his tone turning angry. The government was another favorite topic. "I was up in the night writing letters to some representatives. I thought if your mother knew about it, she might want to do the same."

Birdie blinked at him, wondering anew at his oblivion. Her mother hated politics and never involved herself in anything outside her realm. If it had been her or Sterling who needed medicine, her mother would be a relentless bear, but a stranger child in Kansas wouldn't elicit much interest. Not for the first time Birdie marveled over the many ways her parents were completely different.

"Did she say anything about it?" her father asked.

"No, but I didn't talk much to her this morning," Birdie said. There was a time when she might have pointed out the obvious—that her mother wouldn't, couldn't care about something so far removed from her world, that she had too much on her plate trying to regain the financial years she'd lost being a stay at home mom.

"I'll send you the information. You could write," her father said.

"Okay. I have to go to work. Call if you need anything, all right?" Birdie said. It wasn't a resolution. The hollow sadness was still in his features and would remain there until his mood swung upward again, but at least she had done her duty and tried to make a difference. For all the good it did it felt like raindrops on the ocean.

He nodded and closed the door. Birdie sighed. She would have to talk to Sterling about it, to make him aware of what was happening. The only person who had a remote chance of getting to their dad when he was in his lowest spirals was Sterling. After the divorce, he had become the de facto head of the family, stepping in to make sure both parents were cared for, as well as Birdie.

After rushing to make it on time, Birdie arrived early at work, a fact she realized after she tried the door and found it locked. Shelley was the only one with a key to the building. She checked her phone—ten minutes to wait. The morning was gray and drizzly, but as she stood waiting on the sidewalk the clouds parted and burst open, pouring down a drenching typhoon of rain and wind. Her car was half a block away. She would get soaked trying to make it there. Her best bet was to hug the building behind her, sucking her body close to try and avoid the spray of cold rain.

Something warm and solid touched her wrist and began yanking her. Her head swiveled to the side in time to see Hayden Paxton determinedly tugging her toward his store. He opened the door for her, raising his arm so she could duck inside. He followed her in. The door closed, sealing them inside the quiet warmth of his shop. She should thank him, but she didn't. Instead she began to meander around the shop, looking at the various items on display while he remained in the entryway, watching her.

The shop had been in place for as long as she could remember. It had been his father's shop before his, the place everybody took their everything for repair. If the son was like his father, he also made house calls for appliances. She had been in the store before, when she was a little girl. It was the same as she remembered, with a various and eccentric collection of old clocks and vintage appliances lining the walls and shelves. She paused beside a windup robot that looked like it was from the fifties, wondering if it actually worked. Hayden moved to stand beside her. Reaching for the robot, he wound and set it on the counter where it meandered a short distance before winding down. For some reason they remained there, staring at the motionless robot. Birdie's heart was beating hard. Did he feel the strange tension between them, or was it only her?

She chanced a glance at him but his eyes remained on the robot. His expression was pensive. She wondered what he was thinking. Was he reliving all the times he'd wound this same robot and watched it unwind? The store was still and silent, minus the ticking of the various clocks. Birdie found it soothing. Hayden's eyes slowly left the robot and slid to her. They stared at each other, the easy silence of the store turning heavy and expectant with tension. Slowly, his hand eased toward hers on the desk until, side by side, his index finger reached out to caress hers. Her hand turned slightly, linking her finger with his. Beside them a clock chimed, announcing the hour. Birdie took a step back, turned, and walked outside to her job, her heart pounding hard enough to match the rain.

CHAPTER 6

*W*ork out with us.

BIRDIE STARED AT HER PHONE, wondering why the imperious text came from Duncan and not her brother. Not that Duncan was above trying to order her life; he'd been at it since she met him. But it didn't usually extend to forced workouts.

I'M STILL SORE from yesterday, she replied.

GOOD. I'll pick you up to make sure you don't try to weasel out of it.

SHE ROLLED HER EYES, imagining his face and tone as he sent the text. He was really a pain sometimes and she wasn't in the mood to work out. On the other hand, it would offer a handy distraction from thinking about Hayden. The more she tried to tell herself not to think about him, the more she thought about him. Was he toying with her? That was the only explanation she could come up with for the strange interactions they'd shared. He had to know she was Sterling's little sister. The two had never gotten along. Was she one more pawn in their long running feud?

Birdie was just fastening her hair into a ponytail when Duncan arrived. She had shoulder length naturally curly hair that didn't like to be pinned up. She suspected her ponytail was a mess because it usually was, and her suspicions were confirmed when Duncan stared at it on arrival.

"What?" she asked, her tone defensive as she attempted to smooth the lumps.

"Nothing, I'm used to seeing it down is all," he said. She braced herself for his teasing. When it didn't come she blinked at him in confusion.

"Are you sick?" she asked.

"No," he said, tearing his eyes off her hair as her mother arrived in the room.

"Oh, Duncan," she said, glancing behind him. "Is Sterling here?"

"Hey, Mrs. T. No, I came to drag Birdie into physical fitness, kicking and screaming, if I have to."

"Oh," she said, her smile faltering as her glance bounced between them.

"Want to come with us, Mom?" Birdie offered. Did her mother feel left out? It was the only reason she could think of for her strange expression.

Her mother laughed. "No thanks. I prefer to remain sedentary, thank you very much. You kids, uh, have fun."

"Thanks," Birdie said, giving her a hug before following Duncan to his car.

"Why do you still live with your mom?" he asked as soon as they were backing out the driveway.

"Why not?" Birdie countered, feeling defensive. Duncan had that effect on her after so many years of constant teasing and nitpicking.

"Because you're twenty six. Don't you feel stifled?" he asked.

"Why would I feel stifled? Mom's my best friend, besides Sterling. We do everything together."

"What about dating?"

Her mind flashed to Hayden. What would her mom say if she brought him home? Not that she would because they weren't dating. They'd never even spoken a word to each other. Sterling would have a coronary, not to mention what their father would say if he ever found out.

"Why would Mom care about who I date?" she asked. It was better than telling him it had never come up. Birdie had only had one quasi boyfriend in high school, a prom date that tried to be more for a few weeks before petering out. Since then it hadn't been an issue. She didn't know any eligible men, and she had little time, energy or desire to try and meet someone. Online dating lingered in the back of her mind as a last resort, but she wasn't there yet. And she could only imagine what Duncan would say if she admitted she sometimes thought about putting a profile online in an attempt to snag a man. She shuddered, picturing the teasing such an admission would bring. Or worse, the pity.

"What about you?" she asked.

"I don't live with my parents," he said.

"No, I mean are you dating anyone?" Neither he nor Sterling had ever lacked for female attention. To her knowledge neither had ever gone very long without a girlfriend. But she didn't keep up on Duncan as well as she did her brother. Was he currently attached?

He regarded her with a studying glance. "No, I'm not dating anyone. Not for a while."

"Why not?"

He blew out a breath and faced forward again. "I don't know, Birdie. Lately it's seemed so…dead end and pointless, you know?" He pulled into the gym's parking lot and turned off the car. Birdie remained seated, sensing the conversation wasn't over. "How do you know when you're ready for more?"

"You're asking me for relationship advice? Know your audience, Duncan," she said, poking him.

He batted her hand away with a smile. "Don't you ever feel it, that gaping hole that says something important is missing?"

She froze, considering. Duncan was rarely serious, and especially not with her. In fact this might be the first time they'd ever had a real, non-bickering conversation. "I don't let myself."

"Why not?"

"Because what's the point of yearning for things that are so far out of reach?" she asked.

"Why are they out of reach?" he asked.

"I work three jobs, nearly sixty hours a week, I live," she motioned around them, "here. My parents' marriage was a complete and utter disaster. I'm borderline shy and standoffish with little to no dating history or experience. Where am I going to meet a lifelong love?" Her mind flashed to Hayden and his finger touching hers. With effort, she shoved the memory away.

Duncan stared at her a long minute. He seemed to be thinking, and that alarmed her. He wasn't one for deep thoughts. "I guess you'll have to keep your eyes open in case something sneaks up on you."

"Or I'll go on living my life as I always have, safe, boring, predictable until I die."

He rolled his eyes. "You're twenty six years old, Birdie. Don't be so cynical. It's depressing."

"Pardon me if I don't take life advice from the boy who got so wasted he threw up in my laundry hamper on two separate occasions," she said.

"I was a kid."

"It was two years ago."

He grinned. "A lot can happen in two years."

"Right, you're the pinnacle of maturity now."

His eyes scanned the interior of the gym. "Uh-oh."

"What?" she followed the line of his gaze but couldn't see anything. "She's here."

"Oh," Birdie said. That could only mean one person—Chelsea, Sterling's girlfriend. "What is it with her?"

"She's his girlfriend. I guess it's only natural she'd want to spend time with him."

"No, I mean what is it I don't like about her? I've never been able to put my finger on it."

Duncan let out a sigh. "I don't know but he's pretty serious about her."

"Maybe that's it," Birdie said.

"Maybe what's it?"

"He's never been serious about any of the others. Maybe the fact that he is now is freaking us out. What happens when we're no longer front and center in his life? When he has a wife who comes first?"

"Well, that's depressing. Geez, Birdie, when did you turn into such a downer?" he said, poking her.

"I started out nice and light, but every time someone pokes me I turn darker and more hardened," she said, shoving his finger away.

"You'd think that would work to make me stop poking you, but you'd be wrong," he said, poking her again.

"Why do you love to torture me so?" she asking, pushing his hand away again.

"Good question," he said, his tone suddenly serious.

Birdie faced forward again, blinking in confusion. Lately it seemed like she had no idea what was going on everywhere she went. "I guess we'd better get at it. My muscles aren't going to murder themselves."

"Come on, Chickie. It's leg day," Duncan said, leading the way inside.

"Maybe we could drive through KFC on the way home. Then it could be boneless wing day," she suggested.

He put her in a headlock. "You should have a protein shake and half a banana."

She shoved away from him. "You should have a shower and some stronger deodorant."

"Hey, you're here," Sterling said, blinking in surprise at Birdie.

"I thought you were in on my kidnapping," Birdie said.

"No, it's a complete surprise," Sterling said, his gaze fastening on Duncan who cleared his throat and headed for the weights.

"I guess I'll try the elliptical again," Birdie said. "Hi, Chelsea."

"Hi," Chelsea said.

Birdie could never get a read on her. Did she hate her? Was she standoffish, rude, friendly? Who knew? She never gave anything away, keeping her tone almost robotically neutral whenever they happened to meet. The argument could be made that she was like their mother, stoic and reserved. Sterling tended to be free with both his emotions and his affection, so maybe they balanced each other. But Sterling was so warm, so deeply caring and genuine. Birdie hated the thought of him having to work for anyone's affection. Was Chelsea warmer to him than she was to everyone else? Birdie only wanted the best for him. She wasn't sure Chelsea was it. But she also didn't say so because, close as they were, some topics were still off limits, his girlfriends being chief among them.

"What's up with you and Duncan?" Sterling whispered after having followed her to the elliptical machine.

"Nothing. What are you talking about?" Birdie asked.

"Nothing," Sterling said, his eyes now fastening on his best friend in speculation.

"Did you talk to Dad today?" Birdie asked.

"No, why?"

"He's in a mood," Birdie said.

"A good one or a bad one?"

"Sliding toward bad. There's a sick kid in Kansas."

"Oh, geez," Sterling said, swiping a hand over his face.

"I stopped by this morning, but you know he couldn't care less what I say or do."

"That's not true," Sterling said with zero conviction.

Birdie gave him a look in the floor to ceiling mirror.

"Fine, I'll talk to him, make sure he's doing okay," Sterling promised. He lingered. She could tell he wanted to say more.

"What?"

"Nothing. It's…nothing." He shook his head as if trying to clear it before heading to the weights with Duncan. Chelsea sat on the floor staring at her phone. Apparently they didn't force *her* to workout beyond her will.

The television was on in front of her, some news program. Birdie wanted to change the station, but she didn't know where the remote was. She was scanning the room when the door opened and someone else entered. The mirror in front of her didn't face the door. There was no way to turn and look at the newcomer without being completely obvious, so she had no idea who it was until the treadmill beside her was suddenly taken.

She glanced at Hayden beside her and did a double take. He made no move to look at her or acknowledge her existence. She faced forward, trying to do the same, but it was difficult to think or breathe with him nearby. Was he following her or was it mere coincidence that he showed up when she was working out? And working out with Duncan and her brother, no less. Though if he was merely there to bug them, wouldn't he make some outward sign, flirt with her, talk to her, *look* at her? He did none of those things, however. He set a moderate pace on his treadmill and ran, eyes forward, face totally focused on his workout.

Birdie was about to get off the elliptical and make an escape when Duncan appeared beside her. "Don't be such a wimp, Chickie." He pushed the button on the machine, upping it by three notches. His eyes narrowed and fell on Hayden. "Paxton."

Hayden gave him an upward nod, not speaking or breaking his stride.

With a slight grunt of disgust, Duncan returned to the weights. Birdie began to sweat, struggling against the suddenly torturous machine. It was too hard now, but she would look like a total wimp if she turned it back down. The pain, though. Oh, the pain in her calves. Soon she would sweat so much she would look like a malaria victim. Her hair would kink and curl, shedding its confines like a crab in search of a bigger shell.

Before she could give in and call it quits, Hayden reached over and turned her machine down two notches. The cramping in her calves ceased to be a problem. She smiled. He didn't turn in her direction, but she was almost certain she saw him wink.

ow that you've identified the you you want to be, it's time to get started.

AGAIN WITH THE *YOU YOU*. If it was so easy to figure out who she wanted to be, Birdie wouldn't have needed *Mend Over Matter* to begin with. Why had she bought this stupid book, and why was she still reading it?

Last night she had picked it up again because Duncan's words kept niggling in her brain. *Don't you ever feel it, that gaping hole that says something important is missing?* Yes, she felt it, she had always felt it. But what was the point of feeling it if the solution was so far out of her control? She couldn't make people love her, not potential friends or romantic partners, not even her father. She seemed to be fundamentally lacking in what everyone else was looking for.

Who and what did she want to be?

Maybe it was easier to start with what she wanted: romance and adventure. Her life was sorely lacking in both and always had been. She spent her days planning dream trips filled with both those things, and yet she had never gone anywhere or done anything.

"Why didn't we ever go on vacation?" Birdie was taking her lunch in Sterling's shop. She perched behind the counter and watched him stock shelves while she ate.

"Because Mom and Dad couldn't get along for more than five minutes at a time," he said. "Plus we never had money." Their father tended to spend everything he made on impulse purchases. Since the divorce, her mother had been financially stable for the first time in her adult life, and so had Birdie and Sterling.

"It's kind of an irony I became a travel agent," Birdie said. As a kid she had dreamed of far-flung locales. She still did, but now she realized how much work, planning, and money it took to get to them.

"Hmm," Sterling said, only half listening.

"I want to do something."

"You can help me stock," he offered.

"No, I mean something big, something fun, something crazy."

He paused and looked at her with a smile. "What's crazy for you, Birdie? Rearranging your sock drawer?"

"I want to do something crazy that's not me," she said.

"Like what?"

"That's the problem, I don't know. I feel stagnant, and I hate that."

"You sound like Duncan. He's been beating the same drum."

"Don't you ever feel that way?"

He paused, staring at the box of books at his feet. "Yes."

"What do you do when you feel like that?" she asked.

"Shove it down deep inside and keep working."

"What would you do, if you could do something crazy?" she asked.

"I'd go somewhere and start over," he said.

Her stomach pitched, her heart stopped. "You'd go…away?"

He smiled, but it looked forced. "Of course not. You asked for something crazy. Me going away would be crazy."

"Where would you go?" she asked.

His hand reached up to massage the back of his neck. "Somewhere new where there are no expectations, where no one knows me. No struggling book shop to try and keep afloat. No Mom and Dad to take care of."

She blinked at him, knowing instinctively she was the unspoken part of the sentence. He took care of her, too. He always had. If she had a problem with her car, she called Sterling. If she got locked out of the house, she called Sterling. If she was having a bad day, he was her soft place to fall. She counted on him for everything, and it had never occurred to her until this moment that he might struggle under the weight of so much responsibility, under her.

She finished her meal in silence that went unnoticed by Sterling. When the food was finished, she tidied her space, packed up her container and walked out the door. For once she didn't have to discipline her eyes to stay away from the repair shop. They stayed downcast, fighting tears. She had been rejected by a lot of people but never Sterling. Granted he hadn't rejected her outright. He hadn't said the words, but Birdie had felt them nonetheless. She was a burden on him, a weight, an albatross, the same as their sick dad, the same as his struggling store. Sterling had always been her closest friend. To him she was one more liability.

The travel agency was busy for the rest of the afternoon, and Birdie was thankful. It kept her mind from the new, depressing realization. The one constant in her world had always been Sterling. And now he couldn't be anymore. Who did she have but him? Who had she ever had?

And just like that she identified the *you you* she wanted to be. *I don't want to be alone anymore.*

The day ended and Birdie was dismayed to remember it was her one free night with no other job to rush toward. What would she do with all the endless hours? Watch TV on the couch with her mom? She was twenty six years old. Shouldn't there be more than this? The answer was obviously yes. The problem was that she had no idea how to find anything else. Her own brother wanted to move somewhere to get away from her. What hope did she have of finding a person all her own?

Wearily, she slid behind the wheel of her car and cranked it. Nothing happened. She tried again and three more times. It didn't turn over. She rested her head on the steering wheel. *Now what?*

Before today she would have called Sterling. It was likely she still would, but now she knew the truth. *You're a liability, one more responsibility weighing him down.* Tears flooded her eyes. She sniffed and blinked them back. There was too much of her mom's stoic nature in her to fall apart and have a good cry, but she was close.

A knock sounded on her window. She spun in that direction, startled. Hayden stood on the other side. She rolled down her window. He stuck his hand in and turned the key, listening intently for she knew not what. Satisfied, he turned off the car, opened her door, and popped the hood.

Birdie slid out and stood beside him while he surveyed the engine, occasionally reaching over to touch things. He seemed to come to some conclusion because he closed the hood, took her hand, and led her to his car. Birdie didn't say a word, and neither did he. The silence was both odd and comforting. She should ask what the problem was with her car. She should ask if it was fixable, tell him he didn't have to bother with her. At the very least she should ask him where he was taking her. But she didn't. She sat back and drew a deep breath, inhaling the tangy scent of him that pervaded his car. He glanced at her and smiled, as if he knew what she was doing. She smiled back for no reason whatsoever.

They arrived at the auto parts store. She followed him inside. Once he realized she had followed him, he clasped her hand companionably, and led her to an aisle marked "fuses." He shuffled a few until he located one he wanted and carried it to the counter. Birdie reached for her purse. He waved her away. She drew out her wallet. He ignored her. The clerk rang her up, Hayden presented his credit card. Birdie stuffed a ten dollar bill in his pocket and then blushed when he turned to her with a smile, one eyebrow aloft.

They drove back to her car in silence. She stood by him while he replaced the fuse. He handed her the keys. This time the car started immediately. He closed the hood, walked to her door, and leaned in. She would have to speak this time, would have to thank him. It would be ridiculously rude not to. But before she could do so, he reached across her to the passenger seat, picked up her phone, and typed something in. When that was finished, he handed her the phone, touched his finger to her cheek, and walked away.

A little dazed, Birdie glanced at her phone. Hayden Paxton's number greeted her, front and center. He had programed himself into her contacts. She sent him a text. *Thank you. So much.*

He replied immediately. *You're welcome. So much.*

Smiling now, Birdie started her car and drove home.

irdie thought that was the end of the correspondence, but an hour later her phone buzzed again with another text from Hayden.

Why were you sad after lunch?

She stared at the phone, thinking. How much did she want to tell him about her life? *Have you ever had the sudden realization that you don't mean as much to someone as they do to you?*

Yes.

That's why.

He didn't reply, and she felt foolish. She shouldn't have shared something so personal. On the other hand, *Mend Over Matter* kept telling her to mix it up, to put herself out there. Revealing personal pain to a stranger was definitely outside her comfort zone. With that thought in mind, she reached for the phone again.

What would you do if you did something crazy?

I already did everything crazy. Trying now to do the opposite.

What's crazy to you? I need a frame of reference by which to judge you harshly, she typed, hoping he would catch on to her sense of humor. Sometimes it didn't convey in text.

He replied with a link to a news article, a divorce notice for

Hayden and Kaylee Paxton. He had been married? He was divorced? That explained a lot about his sudden reappearance in town.

I'm so sorry, she replied, feeling it was inadequate.

It has a name, a quick, early relationship without kids. It's called a starter marriage. Sounds hopeful, doesn't it? Felt more like an ending.

Saying I'm sorry again sounds trite, but I really am. I'm sorry for your heart, for the pain of that.

Doesn't sound trite at all. Somehow I think you understand.

I've never been married, she said.

But you've been hurt by someone, he replied and all of a sudden Birdie was crying. Silent tears slipped down her face while a little of the pain eased out of her chest. She hadn't had some big dramatic breakup with a man, but she'd had a series of rejections, first and foremost by her father. And now Sterling, though he hadn't said the words.

Yes.

What's crazy for you? he asked a moment later.

Birdie stared at her phone a moment before typing. *This.* She was sharing her heart with a stranger, and what was most startling was how much she trusted him to keep it safe.

I liked the book, he said, referencing the library book she'd picked for him. *Any other recommendations?*

How much time do you have?

A lot.

I'll put together a list.

How many jobs do you have? he asked.

Three.

Busy girl.

I like it. Leaves less time for shenanigans, she typed.

Shenanigans keep you young, he returned.

Here and there. A steady diet is too much, she said, as if she were some crazy person who grabbed life by the face and didn't let go instead of a mild mannered travel agent/library assistant. *I had to cut back for the sake of my health.*

I know the feeling, he said, and she guessed he probably meant it.

How's your dad? she asked. Five years ago his father had a life-altering stroke. It was the reason he'd given up the repair shop, letting it languish until Hayden came home and took over.

He's okay. It's wrangling with insurance that's the killer. Dad always has a good attitude and likes to be busy, makes it easier.

You sound close.

We are.

What did you do before becoming a repairman?

Fireman.

Really??

Yep.

Why'd you quit?

He took so long to respond she wondered if he wouldn't answer. Eventually he did. *Being a fireman is like being part of a brotherhood. All well and good until one of my "brothers" slept with my wife.*

Wow. Do you have a dog?

?? No, why?

Because dogs provide comfort, and you're in need. Also hugs. Do you have a hugger in your life?

No huggers. Are you volunteering to fill the void?

Her heart fluttered. *Are you text flirting with me?*

I'm everything flirting with you.

She wanted to ask him why. What did he see in her that made him want to reach out? The little insecure part of her said it was because of Sterling and the long running feud, but surely not. Surely someone who was so recently heartbroken wouldn't be so heartless. Would he?

She realized she hadn't responded to his last text in some time. How best to answer those provocative little words?

Cute.

Me or the flirting? he replied.

Everything, she said. The anonymity of texting made her brave. She would never tell a man in real life she thought he was cute.

Back at you, he said and she smiled stupidly at her phone, hugging it tightly to her chest.

CHAPTER 9

A few mornings later Birdie received a text from Sterling.

Dinner with Dad tonight and I need a buffer. His house at 6.

She didn't reply, and he didn't seem to notice. Of course she would go. It seemed as if for once he actually needed her for something. The last few days she had tried to give him a reprieve, to limit her dependence and contact. Their parents hadn't done the same. Their mom had called three times with car and house issues and their dad had apparently been in contact, too.

That morning Birdie woke early to get ready. It was the day she was supposed to pick up the clock from Hayden, and she wanted to look good. Something had shifted between them, had morphed from odd chemistry to shared information.

Now she stared critically at herself in the mirror, assessing her reflection. She wasn't ugly. She was just...there. Her features weren't unpleasant, but neither were they arranged in that mysteriously spectacular way that equaled beauty. Makeup had never appealed to her. Every time she tried to wear it in the past she ended up feeling somehow less authentic and overly made up, as if she were trying to be someone she wasn't. Plus her complexion was her best feature. It seemed a shame to cover it under layers of blush, powder and foundation. Today she put on eye makeup and was surprised by the difference it made. The mascara made her eyes pop and stand out and she began to believe it was her technique that had been lacking and not makeup itself.

Her hair was another bothersome matter. It was so curly it did its own thing and she let it, as if they had some sort of prearranged agreement that let them go their separate ways. Before she could talk herself out of it, she reached for her blow-dryer and began the arduous task of straightening, adding several inches of length when it was finished.

Next she reached for a skirt and sweater. Thanks to her frequent workouts the last couple of weeks, her body had toned somewhat, causing the clothes to conform nicely to her shape. She stared at the finished product in the mirror, for once with approval. The person who stared back at her looked different, more mature and put together, the sort of woman who would be carrying out a secret flirtation with a handsome man. Perhaps the knowledge of that secret gave her an extra confidence.

Shelley said nothing when Birdie arrived at work, easing her. The last thing she wanted was to look like she was trying too hard.

"I'm picking up the clock at lunch today," Birdie announced.

"Hmm?" Shelley said, lowering her untouched mug of coffee from her lips.

"The clock." Birdie pointed to the empty spot on the wall. "It's ready today."

"Oh, right. I can pick it up. I hate for you to have to do that."

"I really don't mind," Birdie said.

Shelley looked up again, blinking slowly. "Oh. I see. Let me get you the company card." She retrieved the credit card and laid it on Birdie's desk.

"Thank you," Birdie muttered, studiously ignoring her as she focused hard on her computer.

The hours until lunch seemed to drag. At last it was noon. Birdie ducked into the bathroom, checking her hair and makeup, and headed next door. Her hand was on the door of the shop when a new voice spoke.

"What are you doing?" Duncan asked.

Birdie dropped her hand and faced him "What?"

Duncan stopped short, pausing mid step. "Whoa. Are you going to prom?"

"Don't be silly. I wear skirts all the time," Birdie said, smoothing it.

"It's not the skirt. It's the face and hair. I didn't know you could get it this straight." He touched the ends of her hair.

She batted his hand away. "I was in the mood for change."

"Huh." His continued unblinking assessment of her was making her nervous. And she was acutely aware they were having the conversation on the other side of Hayden's door, likely in his full view.

Duncan seemed to come to the same realization because he dragged his attention away from her in order to scowl through the door. "I wanted to see if you were up for lunch today."

"Just you and me?"

"Too weird?" he said, smiling.

"No, but," her eyes turned helplessly toward Hayden's shop. "I need to pick up a clock for work."

"I'll go with you," Duncan said, opening the door for her.

Birdie ducked inside, tamping down her frustration. Hayden stood behind the counter surveying them with a half smile. To Birdie it looked half-amused and half-annoyed.

Turning, he reached back and produced her clock, resting it on the counter between them. Duncan hovered by the door. Birdie hadn't turned to check, but she was pretty sure he was scowling.

Birdie produced her credit card and pressed it into Hayden's palm. He rang her up and handed her the receipt to sign. She signed and handed it back. Their fingers brushed unnecessarily during the hand-off. She met his eyes and they exchanged a slow smile.

"Ready?" Duncan asked. His terse tone burst the bubble of expectant tension.

"Yes," Birdie said, her gaze unwavering on Hayden.

Duncan eased forward and picked up the clock. "Come on."

Birdie backed up a step, reluctant to break eye contact with Hayden.

"Can you get the door?" Duncan asked, annoyed with her slowness.

At last she turned, opened the door, and followed him through.

"Man, I hate that guy," he muttered as they deposited the clock next door.

"Why?" Birdie asked.

"We've been over this," he said. He hung the clock back on the wall and held the door for her.

"Only for Sterling's benefit? Because of some high school feud?"

"No. He was always so…I mean, you saw the way he was just now, standing there with that dumb, provoking grin. He always acts like he's superior, like he has secret information."

"Maybe he's merely quiet, a man of few words," Birdie suggested.

Duncan shook his head and surprised her by slipping his arm around her and squeezing her shoulders. "You're too nice, Birdie. You never see the bad in anyone." His arm remained on her shoulders until they arrived at his car. He held the door for her and she slid inside. Her phone buzzed.

What was with the bodyguard? Hayden texted.

No idea. He met me outside and asked to have lunch. Sorry. Why was she sorry? She had no idea, but it was too late to take it back.

No biggie. Just be careful with that guy.

. . .

SHE ALMOST LAUGHED. *It's only Duncan, my brother's best friend.*

I KNOW DUNCAN, *and I'm telling you to be careful. His reputation precedes him.*

SHE FROWNED, not certain she liked Hayden saying things about Duncan. *I'm aware, but it doesn't extend to me. He sees me as his kid sister.*

MAYBE HE USED TO. *Not anymore.*

BIRDIE TURNED to study Duncan who was busy pulling onto the roadway. He caught sight of her staring. "What?"

"Nothing."

"Who are you texting?"

"A friend."

He laughed as if the thought of her having a friend he was unaware of was a big joke. "What friend?"

"You don't know everyone I know. I have a life." She didn't, but she could. Just because he was Sterling's friend didn't mean he knew everything about her.

He frowned.

Her phone buzzed again. *Rain check on that hug?*

Birdie glanced at Duncan again. If he knew she was texting Hayden, he'd be livid.

Absolutely, she replied before tucking her phone in her purse.

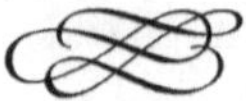

CHAPTER 10

"I'm worried about Sterling."

Duncan had been unusually quiet since he picked Birdie up, and that worried Birdie for reasons she couldn't articulate. But with Sterling on the agenda, they were back on even footing.

"Why?" she asked.

"He's been tense, withdrawn, preoccupied. Haven't you noticed?"

"No, I've been giving him space."

"Why?"

Birdie sighed. "Come on, Duncan. You know how it is."

"How is it?"

"Everyone depends on Sterling, Mom, Dad, me. He's the glue that keeps our family together. Sometimes it has to be too much."

"Come on, Birdie. You know he loves you."

"I do, and I love him. That's why I've been giving him a break from me."

He blinked at her in consternation. "That's a terrible thing to say."

"But not untrue. Sterling needs to live his own life, and if I can figure out how to live mine, it's one less albatross for him to contend with."

He huffed. "Albatross. You are no one's albatross."

"Aren't I? He's been in charge of me for as long as I can remember, running interference with Dad, defending me, protecting me, drawing me out. Being my brother, my parent, my best friend. It's too much." Her eyes filled with tears. She didn't say what she was really thinking, that *she* was too much.

"Birdie, stop, you're being crazy."

She swiped her nose with a tissue. "Perfect, Duncan, pile it on."

"I didn't mean that literally. I meant your current line of thinking is out of order. Your parents are maybe sometimes too much to handle, your dad especially. But you're not like that. You're not needy or clingy. You're fun and sweet and supportive. Sterling does not view you as a liability any more than he views me as one."

Birdie made no reply to that. He meant it nicely, she was sure, but Duncan *was* a bit of a liability. He was possessive of Sterling, jealous of other friends, girlfriends, even Birdie at times. As much as he didn't want to see it, Duncan depended on Sterling as much as everyone else did. Sterling was their alpha, the leader of their pack. Duncan liked to believe he was an alpha too, but he wasn't. He was a beta, just like Birdie, at least compared to Sterling.

"We're having dinner with Dad tonight. I'll try to assess Sterling then," Birdie promised.

"Why *do* you look so nice today?" Duncan pressed.

She glanced down self-consciously. "I'm a tad insulted you think I look that different than normal."

"No, it's not…You're a cute kid, Birdie. Pretty easy on the eyes, better with age and all that. But today," he reached for her hand and gave it a squeeze, "kind of a hottie."

She tugged her hand free, flustered. "I feel like I'm getting the full Duncan Shepherd treatment, and I'm so confused right now."

"What's to be confused about? You're an attractive woman, I'm an insanely handsome man. We're having lunch, the end."

"You're a player and we annoy each other greatly."

"Do we?" he said, taking a long sip of his drink while he eyed her.

"Yes, we do," she replied, taking an equally long sip while she returned his stare. "And you're still a player."

"Lonely tigers change their stripes," he said in a tone that bordered on embarrassed. Birdie frowned and continued sipping, not sure how to respond. This was *Duncan.* It wasn't like that with him, hadn't ever been. If something was going to develop between them, shouldn't it have been when they were both pubescent and he spent every waking moment at her house while she walked around in pajamas in all her teenage glory? Why now, a decade later, did he appear to be hitting on her?

Objectively, he was a catch. He was overtly handsome and had a solid, well-paying job. He owned his own house and drove a nice car. He was the sort of man who was nice to date over Valentine's Day because he always remembered to send flowers or buy presents or send a card. But there were messy parts of him, pieces of his adolescence he hadn't yet been able to put away. He still liked to drink and party, much more than Birdie was comfortable with. He put too much stock in appearances, body size and clothing especially. Most problematic of all was the fact that he always thought he was right and tended to take over whenever they were together, telling her what to do and how to live much more than Sterling ever had. Physically, he was appealing. Emotionally, she wasn't at all certain of him.

"You're staring at me," he said, smiling in the cocky way she didn't like.

"I'm trying to figure something out."

"What?"

"Whether the unlikable parts of you are due to immaturity or bad character."

He sucked a breath. "Ouch."

She shrugged. "You're like my family, Duncan. If I can't be honest with you, who can I be honest with?"

"Fine, then let me reciprocate. You're serious and uptight and borderline boring. But I think, given the chance, we could have something, and I think, given the chance, it could be something good."

"What does Sterling think about that statement?"

He shrugged. "I didn't run it by him."

"You don't think he'd like to have input on the possibility of us?" she asked.

"If there's a possibility of us, his input is none of our concern."

She blinked at him, surprised. "Wow."

"Nothing's happened between us. Maybe nothing will. All I'm saying is think about it," he said. "Can you do that?"

"I can do that," she said.

"Good." He smiled at her in a way he never had before, flirtatiously, and Birdie felt her stomach flutter in response. He was a handsome man, ridiculously so, with the sort of over-the-top lush features that would have been girly on anyone less masculine. Birdie had always prided herself on her immunity to him. While other girls fawned, she had been impervious. *It's just Duncan, my brother's obnoxious best friend.* She had never once, in her entire life, felt an iota of interest or attraction for him. Until today.

"Huh," she said.

"What?"

"This day isn't turning out at all like I thought," she said.

"How did you think it would turn out?" he asked.

With Hayden sitting where you are. She hadn't lacked purpose when she decided to pick up the clock at lunch time. But instead of having lunch with Hayden like she hoped, she was having lunch with Duncan, and it was nice. And now she was confused.

He dropped her at work, walked her to the door of the travel agency, and leaned in to kiss her cheek. "Think about it," he commanded.

"I'll ponder," she said, standing on her toes to kiss his cheek in return. Now it was his turn to look at her in surprise. She had never been overtly physically affectionate with him before. She'd tossed him a few pity hugs over the years, when he was feeling low. Occasionally she put him in a headlock, but in most instances she was so annoyed she was actually trying to choke him. Even when she graduated high school and he performed the same sort of cheek kiss he'd just done, she had returned the favor grudgingly, as if under duress. Then she had been embarrassed, had given some typically awkward teenage maneuver like push him away or muss his hair after the deed was done. Now she returned his gaze unblinking until he was the first to look away, his cheeks slightly flushed.

"See you, Birdie."

"See you, Duncan."

She turned and went inside her building, not staying still to watch him walk away.

* * *

HER FATHER HADN'T SHOWERED. There was nothing surprising about that. Sometimes when he was in one of his lows, hygiene took a back seat. What was surprising to Birdie was that Sterling appeared to have skipped the shower, too, and that was highly unlike him.

"Did you come from working out?" she asked him.

"No," he said, not volunteering any further explanation.

"It's good you're keeping up on your workouts," their dad interjected. "Don't want to get soft." He was soft with a slightly paunchy belly. Birdie was never certain if his warnings were a cautionary tale of what might happen or if he was so wholly out of touch he didn't realize he'd gone soft long ago.

"Birdie's been working out, too," Sterling volunteered.

"Huh," her dad said, not bothering to look up from his plate. Birdie tossed Sterling a smile. Short of winning a Heisman trophy, Birdie had zero chance of ever getting her father's attention or approval. Everything had always been about Sterling—his sports prowess, his popularity, his good grades and high IQ. Outside of good grades Birdie had never given him much to be proud of, but why did she have to? Shouldn't he love her because she was his daughter?

Shoving aside the old resentment, she made herself focus on the present. As Duncan had said, Sterling was tense, distracted, and stressed. *What's wrong with you?* she mouthed over the table.

He shook his head, frowning.

Birdie frowned in return. Their father bumbled on, oblivious to anything but his own feelings and words, as usual. "Everything would have been different if you'd gotten that scholarship senior year. You wouldn't be working out for nothing. You might have gone pro."

Sterling's hand tensed on his water glass. "I wouldn't have gone pro, Dad. I wasn't that good."

"You don't know how good you might have been if you'd played in college. It's all because of that Paxton boy."

Birdie jumped, knocked into her water glass, and grabbed it at the last second, sloshing a few drops on her hand. She opened her mouth to apologize to her dad before realizing he hadn't noticed because, as usual, he wasn't looking at her. *Why am I here?* she mouthed to Sterling who smiled and shook his head at her. She put her arms up and began moving them back and forth, along with her head, miming an Egyptian. Her dad continued his rant about Sterling's missed chances while Sterling stared at her and tried hard not to laugh.

"You could still try," their dad finished and both of them tuned in, belatedly realizing they had no idea what he'd been saying.

"Try what, Dad?" Sterling asked.

"Try out for pro ball. They have some events like those, open to unknown rookies."

"It's true, I saw a movie about it," Birdie added. "This golden retriever was able to walk on mid season and become quarterback."

Sterling snickered, unable to hold back his laughter anymore. Their dad finally looked at her, to scowl. "That's not funny."

"It actually is, Dad," Sterling said. "And it's completely unrealistic. NFL teams do not take walk-ons and, even if they did, I am not good enough to play. I'm not even certain I would have been good enough for a scholarship, nor that I would have wanted to continue playing after high school." He rubbed the area between his eyes, looking tired. "Besides, Hayden Paxton is back here now, working at his dad's shop right next to mine. Getting that scholarship didn't seem to do him any favors in life."

"He didn't have as much potential as you do. If you'd have gotten that scholarship..."

"But I didn't," Sterling exclaimed, startling their father and Birdie who jumped, bumping her water again. Sterling didn't have outbursts.

He always put up with their father's spiels, listening patiently and then pushing them aside like yesterday's leftovers.

Their dad shut down, withdrawing into his cocoon of wounded feelings. Birdie waited for Sterling to apologize, as he usually did if he said something to upset their dad. The minutes ticked and he said nothing. Awkwardness stretched and grew, casting a pall over the dinner.

"Who do we like for the Super Bowl this year?" Birdie tried.

"It's not who we like so much as who has a lock on it. The cheaters, as usual," her dad said. After a minute long rant about cheaters he picked up the thread of football again and carried on a one sided conversation. Sterling caught her eye over the table. *Thanks,* he mouthed.

I'm worried about you, she said.

I'm fine, he assured her but the tired set of his features and the worry lines around his eyes said something different. He was not fine. Birdie had no idea what might be bothering him. Previous to this week she would have said they shared everything with each other. But after learning Sterling dreamed of escape, she wasn't so certain. What was happening with him that was eating him up inside? How could she find out, and was there anything she could do to help?

The questions replayed themselves in her mind as she arrived home and fielded her mother's questions about the evening. Despite the fact that her mother had never discouraged her from having a relationship with her dad, Birdie maintained a strange sense of disloyalty whenever they got together. Her relationship with her father was tenuous and difficult. He had walked out on their mother, on them, was emotionally untethered and hard to communicate with, let alone love. But he was still her father and she still had to try with him. Didn't she? Yet every time she went for a meal at his house she felt like she was abandoning her mom, choosing sides where there weren't supposed to be any sides. After a few years of acrimony, her parents had arrived at a peaceful stalemate. They could communicate now without arguing or throwing blame. Everything had settled down, but for Birdie the feelings never went away—the sorrow, the loss, the helplessness and insecurity.

Her phone buzzed with a text from Hayden.

What did you do tonight?

Family dinner. Kill me now. What did you do?

Worked on my car.

Is your car having trouble? she asked.

No, it's a different car. I'm restoring an old Mustang.

Ooo, nice. Picture?

He sent her a picture of a primer gray vintage Mustang. *The paint job comes last. I'm thinking red.*

I'm thinking red is perfect. Is it to sell or keep?

Keep. I'm planning a big trip.

She settled onto her bed cross-legged. *Did someone say trip? I might know a good travel agent. Where are you going?*

. . .

THE PACIFIC COAST HIGHWAY.

NO WAY. That sounds amazing. I've planned a few trips there. I'm available to help, if you need it. No pressure, I'm not trying to insert myself into your dream trip.

I WOULD LOVE THE HELP, and I want you to insert yourself. In fact...

THE THREE LITTLE dots came up and lingered but nothing else was forthcoming.

IN FACT WHAT? she asked at last, unable to take the suspense any longer.

I WAS GOING to say maybe you could go with me, but we're not there yet.

IT DOESN'T HAVE to be a romantic venture. It could be a Thelma and Louise *thing as we both flee our troubled lives. And the law.*

NOW YOU'RE TALKING. Dibs on being Thelma.

I HAD dibs on you being Brad Pitt.

LOL. I should have guessed you were kind of rotten. It's always the quiet ones you have to watch out for.

. . .

Guess that means I have to watch out for you, too.

Absolutely.

She frowned at the phone, not sure how to take that statement. *Do you miss being a firefighter?*

Sometimes. I miss the adrenaline rush, miss helping people. It's nice to have regular hours now, but not very exciting.

You could volunteer, she suggested.

Maybe someday. I don't do well with meeting new people, takes me a while to warm up. Volunteering is different than working. More social pressure on the volunteer to be open and chatty.

I've never considered that before, but I can see it. Which is probably why I don't volunteer for anything. Should probably make that a New Year's Resolution, to reach out and touch someone.

I'm on my way, he said. She laughed, thinking he was joking until about ten minutes later he texted again.

Come outside.

. . .

HEART THRUMMING, she skipped down the hallway and opened the door. Hayden stood on the porch. He grasped her hand, pulled her close, and hugged her tightly. Birdie returned his hug, resting her head on his chest as her arms slid around his middle. They stood together clutching tightly for a long time until at last he kissed the top of her head, let her go, and walked away without a word.

ell me something.

Birdie's phone buzzed with a text from Hayden first thing the next morning.

What should I tell? she replied.

Something I don't know about you.

That would be everything.

Fair point, he conceded. *Tell me something no one knows about you.*

Birdie thought long and hard about that. There were few things Sterling and their mother didn't know about her. Only one thing came to mind, really.

When my parents were going through their divorce, I imagined my dad was dead. It was easier to believe he died than that he willingly didn't want us anymore.

She hit "send" before carefully thinking it through and had immediate regrets. *Yikes, that was a downer, sorry.*

I never said it had to be peppy. And the truth is I used to do the same about my wife. Lying to myself. The real truth is that I still do. Much easier than thinking of her with someone not me.

The text came through and then he added his own addendum. *Well, that escalated quickly. Sorry to spew.*

She smiled at her phone. *It's fine. You're in a raw place right now, I get it. It seems like this might be what I'm here for, to receive and manage the spew.*

Like a garbage collector for texts, he replied.

Exactly, but without the high salary and cool perks.

If you're my therapist, does that make it unethical if I continue to flirt with you? he asked.

I demand it, she replied, and he sent her a winking emoji.

I'm not an emoji kind of guy, am I?

You can be anything. The beauty of starting over, she said, her glance falling on the self-help book she still hadn't finished. Who would she be, if she started over? Who did she want to be now?

I like that mighty fine, he replied, adding another winking emoji along with the one with hearts for eyes. *Sorry. I'm new at these. I'll practice.*

I like them mighty fine, she replied, and he sent her a smiling emoji. She sent him a fist, followed by a robot.

Are you trying to tell me you want to punch a robot?

She rolled her eyes. *No, I was fist bumping you and sending you a robot to remind you of the one in your dad's store.*

I love that robot, he said.

I know, she replied, and he sent another winking emoji.

"Yo."

Birdie looked up to the open doorway of her bedroom. Duncan leaned his shoulder on the jamb.

"Are you channeling Rocky?" she asked.

"Adrian," he said, pulling his mouth askew in an eerily adept Sylvester Stallone imitation. Without invitation, he walked in and sat beside her on her bed, scanning her room. "Not sure I've ever been in here before sober."

"Thanks for the reminder," she said. Her room was by the bathroom. On two separate occasions he had stumbled in and drunkenly thrown up in her hamper. The memory was doubly unpleasant because, confronted with his misdeed, he had laughed. Hard. Birdie'd had to buy a new hamper. Twice.

"What are you doing here?" she asked.

He shrugged a shoulder. "Stopping by. It's a thing people do when they're considering going out. I tell you this because you are lacking in experience and in need of instruction." He turned to grin at her.

"I may be a rookie, but I'm fairly certain dropping by unannounced and plunking yourself in the woman's bedroom is not on the list of recommended behavior," she said.

"How about this," he said and, before she could understand what he was doing, bridged the gap between them and kissed her. Birdie was too shocked to think about the ramifications. All she knew was that it had been a long time since someone kissed her, and no one had ever done it so well. Her fist knotted in his shirt, drawing him closer, while his hand tangled in her hair, tipping her face in order to deepen the kiss.

A sound from the living room alerted them to the fact that her mother was home and could walk in on them at any moment. Duncan pulled away, his hand attempting to smooth her flyaway curls. "And that is why you need your own place."

"Did you kiss me to prove a point?" she asked.

"Yes, but not that one," he said.

"Which one?" she asked. It was hard to focus on his words. Her hand was still tangled in his shirt—for support, she now realized. He had made her limp, Duncan of all people.

"That you and I work together," he said. And then he kissed her again, advancing on her until she was pressed against the headboard of her bed. Her leg started to curl around his, and she realized what was happening. *He is devouring me.* She put up a hand, leaning away from him slightly as she gave him a light shove.

"I feel like we've skipped a few steps," she said, embarrassed by how near to breathless she sounded. And felt. She was glad for the support of the headboard, apparently the only thing now keeping her upright. Because she'd been kissed incoherent. By *Duncan.*

"How so?" he asked. He was smug, and she didn't like it. She put her knees up, creating a safety barrier between them.

"Like a sweet first kiss to test the waters. You jumped straight to can-I-get-pregnant-from-a-kiss level."

He snorted and swiped a hand over his eyes. "Geez, Birdie. We've known each other all our lives. I thought that bought me a little leeway."

Did it? Did she want Duncan to kiss her? Clearly a part of her did. He was ridiculously good at it, but she could have guessed that about him. It would be impossible not to be so, what with all the practice he'd had.

"Why are you scowling at me?" he asked, reaching out to smooth the crease between her brows.

"You're confusing me."

"What's confusing? I've put a lot of thought into this. We know everything about each other. Your dark secrets are totally livable, as are your vices and annoying bad habits. The only question was whether or not we had chemistry." He leaned forward, whispering. "And we do, Birdie, we do."

Drat him, he was making her fluttery. She put her hands on his chest and gave him a light shove again. "Maybe you've thought through the ramifications, but I haven't."

"What's to think about?" he asked. He meant it as cocky as it sounded, she was certain. It would never occur to him that she might refuse him, that she might, in fact, have other offers. Though, did she? Hayden was clearly still mourning his failed marriage.

"A lot, Duncan. Give me some time to catch up."

He gave a longsuffering sigh. "Take a leap, Birdie. Not everything has to be so safe all the time."

"Worst case scenario, we try this and it ends badly, then what?" she asked.

"Then it's awkward when we see each other, but how often is that, really? Here and there when our paths intersect. Sterling's wedding day will be a pain, but we'll manage. Now let me ask you a question: best case scenario, we try this and it ends beautifully, then what?"

"I think that's still a question for you. What does it look like if it ends beautifully?" she asked, genuinely curious. What sort of future was he envisioning for them?

He wagged his eyebrows, then leaned forward and kissed her again, softly and sweetly. This time she didn't push him away. The kiss ended and they rested their foreheads together. "There is something good to be said for starting at the beginning, baby girl," he murmured. He kissed her forehead and walked out of her room, leaving her staring after him in dismay.

CHAPTER 12

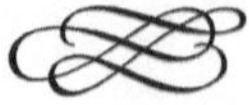

ow that you've identified the you you want to be, it's time to say the words out loud. Too often we keep things in our heads for fear of being rejected. No more fear! Say it loud and proud!

"I DON'T WANT to be alone." Birdie whispered the words, but even so they felt impactful. This was the *you you* she had chosen, not to be alone. And then, so quick she was left surprised and breathless, she added more words, "And I want to take chances." Where had that come from?

Being with Duncan checked both those boxes. It would alleviate the problem of being alone, and it would be a risk, the riskiest sort of risk because it was not only risking her heart, it was risking her relationship with her brother. There could be fallout with Sterling if things with Duncan went awry. Did she even want to be with Duncan? She had no idea. Those kisses, though… And what about Hayden? Where did he fit into all of this? As if sensing she was thinking about him, her phone beeped with a text.

. . .

Just saw Mr. Benson. That guy must be 10,000 years old.

She reached for her phone, picturing their former high school math teacher, Mr. Benson. Her fingers intended to text some quippy reply about his advanced age. What she sent instead was, *Duncan kissed me.*

A text bubble appeared and disappeared three times before he finally answered.

What?

I don't know.

Why are you telling me?

She stared off into space, thinking. *Because it seems like whatever this is is honest, and I want to keep it that way. Most of all because I'm confused and have no one else to tell.*

Looks like I'm here to manage your spew, too, he typed.

Looks like. Sorry.

Okay, here goes. Did you want him to kiss you?

. . .

No.

Did you tell him to stop?

Ineffectually, yes.

Did you like it after the fact?

Yes, she replied, blushing. *But I probably would have regardless. Not a lot of experience in these matters. Clearly.*

There's no way to say this without sounding like a jealous guy you're texting, but you need to be careful with him. I don't think it's a good idea for you to be with him.

I'm not sure I do either, but I'd like to hear your why, she replied.

In third grade, he pulled Lisa McKinney's dress over her head, showed the class her underpants, and made her cry.

Birdie stared at her phone. *That's it? I'm going to need more than a twenty-year-old anecdote.*

It's not a twenty-year-old anecdote; it's one of many anecdotes. Duncan is not nice.

. . .

Birdie reviewed everything she knew about Duncan. *Sometimes he is.*

Is that enough for you? Hayden asked.

Was it? She didn't answer that question. *Sometimes people change, sometimes they mature.*

People don't change. They only become more of what they already were, he replied.

Insightful, but I'm no less confused. What she wanted, she now realized, was some sort of declaration from him, some sign that this weird thing they had going on was more than it was, that he wanted to be with her the way Duncan wanted to be with her.

Just be careful, he said in reply. Birdie was glad they weren't conversing in person so she didn't have to try and hide her disappointment. Of course there was nothing between them. They were strangers. They had never even spoken a word to each other, and they certainly hadn't kissed. She and Duncan had decades of history together and proof positive that there was actual chemistry between them. She'd be crazy not to act on that for the sake of something not real. Right?

Thanks, she belatedly replied, hoping her disappointment didn't convey.

· · ·

HIS TEXT BUBBLE popped up and disappeared three more times before he finally answered. *You can talk to me. We're...friends?*

TEXT FRIENDS?

TENDS? he offered.

FRIEXTS, she returned and he sent her a smiling emoji in return. *It goes both ways,* she added. *I meant what I said about managing the spew. If you need to talk about things, to work through them, I'm here.*

THANKS, he replied.

IT WAS her day off from the travel agency, but not the library. After Duncan's abrupt insertion into her life and thoughts, it would be a relief to face the quiet of the library. Or so she thought. Really, it left her alone with her thoughts. She stared hard at her phone, willing Hayden to text. He hadn't since that morning. Was he avoiding her now? Was whatever was between them gone for good? If so, she really had no excuse not to be with Duncan. Was she looking for an excuse not to be with Duncan?

"I want to take chances," she whispered and sent Hayden a text.

TELL me about the robot in your dad's store.

THE THOUGHT BUBBLES popped up and disappeared again a few times. Was he trying to frame a reply or looking for a way to tell her to buzz off?

. . .

My DAD IS *the keeper of lost things, old ways of doing things as well as broken things that need to be fixed. Things have a way of appearing in the store and never going away again. I loved it when I was a kid, it was the ultimate safe place, filled with fascinating things and the comfort to explore them. No idea where the robot came from, I doubt my dad even remembers. But it's always been there, and I always played with it, winding it up and letting it wind itself down. It made me feel...*the text bubbles disappeared a few times before he continued. *Melancholy? But also hopeful somehow. No matter how many times that dumb robot stopped moving, all I had to do was wind it up again. Kind of a metaphor for my life. The divorce, the job loss, the move—they all took a toll. Coming home was like inserting the key in my back. I guess I'm looking for something to wind me up again.*

BIRDIE SAT STARING at her phone a long time.

TOO MUCH SPEW? Hayden asked after a while.

NO, too much good stuff to process in a short amount of time. I think I'm the robot sitting on the shelf, waiting to be picked up. I've never found my key, never been wound up, but somehow I know those things are supposed to happen.

THE ROBOT WORKS on so many levels, Hayden said.

IT REALLY DOES, she agreed. *Though usually a robot is used to represent someone without a heart or brain, a mindless, unfeeling automaton.*

. . .

MAYBE IN THIS case it represents two people who've been hurt so bad they've put their hearts and minds on pause and are waiting for it to be safe enough to restart them again.

YOU'RE all kinds of deep, Hayden Paxton.

ONLY WITH YOU, Birdie Thompson.

SHE CLUTCHED her phone and asked the thing she most wanted to ask. *Do you hate my brother?*

THE THOUGHT BUBBLES did their disappearing act a few times again before he answered. *Yes.*

IS that why you're talking to me? To annoy him and Duncan?

NO. Ten years ago, it might have been. Now I have no energy for feuds.

SHE BLINKED AWAY HER TEARS. Why was she crying? She had no idea. Forcing herself to say the next part, she did it quickly before she could lose her nerve. *Why do you hate him?*

YOU DON'T WANT to know.

IF I DIDN'T, I wouldn't have asked, she returned.

· · ·

THE THOUGHT BUBBLES worked so long she thought he wouldn't reply for sure this time. Eventually, he did. *He's not real.*

BIRDIE WAS ABOUT to put him on blast. How dare he say that about her beloved brother? Then, miraculously, she deleted the angry text and sent an inquiring one instead, feeling disloyal the entire time. *Why?* Hayden had shown great insight into things in her life. Maybe his take on Sterling would give her a better perspective on him, too.

STERLING HAS ALWAYS BEEN EXACTLY who everybody wanted him to be, never himself.

IT WAS TRUE, Sterling was the ultimate people pleaser. *Maybe so, but not for selfish purposes. He likes to take care of people.*

MAYBE SO, Hayden conceded. *But if he's always being a different person for everyone in his life, who is he?*

WHY DOES IT BOTHER YOU?

BECAUSE I SEEMED to be the only one who could see through the façade. And that's why he doesn't like me, FYI. Because I know the truth—he's not as perfect as he seems. The funny part is that I'd probably like him better if he'd stop trying to be Mr. Wonderful all the time.

I'VE RECENTLY DISCOVERED I'm one of his liabilities, she text blurted. What was wrong with her? She never told people this much about herself.

Yet she couldn't stop word vomiting all over Hayden Paxton. *The anonymity of text is clearly giving me loose lips.*

HE SENT her two winking emojis. **Those are for the loose lips reference* It loses something when you have to explain. Anyway, after the last few years of not being able to discuss anything with my cheating wife and cheating best friend, it feels kind of great to know I can say anything and you're doing the same. And it's kind of my personality to say whatever I'm thinking. A fact that is usually harsher and off putting in real life.*

I'M TRYING to imagine you saying these things in real life, but all I can come up with is you making the emoji winking faces in real life.

STOP NOW. DO NOT PICTURE ME MAKING EMOJI WINKING FACES. I EXPRESSLY FORBID IT.

STOP YELLING, Grandpa.

SORRY I HAD to be forceful. Back to Sterling. When someone sees himself as a savior, everyone is in need of being saved. After a while it must become exhausting. Try not to take it personally.

BUT I DO TAKE it personally. He's always been my best friend. To know that's not reciprocal is...painful. Without Sterling, I'm truly on my own.

NOT SO. Hello? Someone knocked on the counter in front of her face. Birdie looked up to see Hayden smiling at her, phone in hand.

· · ·

"Oh," she gasped, and then pressed her lips together, feeling that talking would somehow ruin what was between them. Hayden leaned over the counter, pulled her into a hug, and held her close for a minute, resting his head on hers. She returned the hug, squeezing him tight. It might have gone on forever, but the library's front door opened.

Hayden let her go and disappeared into the stacks. And now Duncan stood before her. "Hey."

She blinked at him, surprised. "You know this is a library, right?"

He made a show of looking around. "So this is what one looks like. What's that weird smell?"

"Knowledge," she returned, and he flicked her hand where it rested on the counter. "What are you doing here?"

"Why do you keep questioning me? I'm making appearances," he said. He leaned against the counter, smiling. "Looks like we're alone."

"We're not. Someone is in the stacks," Birdie said.

"Ah. And that's why you're nervously hedging away from me," he said.

Birdie blew out a breath and pushed her hair out of her face. "I need space and time to think."

"I don't," he said.

"I think you're supposed to give me space and time when I request them," she said.

"Why? I don't agree with it. There's nothing to think about. If I leave you alone, you'll overthink. It's a thing with you," he said, rolling his eyes.

"That's kind of annoying."

"What?"

"That you don't listen to me when I talk and that you think you know me so well."

"I do know you so well," he said

"You don't."

"I do. Test me." He spread his feet apart and crossed his arms in his defensive basketball pose.

"What's my favorite book?" she tried.

"Something girly, probably. Who cares?"

"I care. Hello, I work in a library," she spread her hands wide.

"That's not who you are, it's what you like."

"How is it different?" she asked.

"It just is. What's the big deal? We know the fundamentals," he said.

"Do we? I've never even seen where you live."

He perked up. "You wanna come over? Let's go."

Hayden returned and set a large stack of books on the counter, forcing Duncan aside. Duncan eyed the stack critically. "Since when are you such a bookworm, Paxton?"

"Kindergarten," Hayden replied. "Your observation skills, not so sharp apparently." He fished for his library card, but Birdie was already scanning him.

"You're really going to read," Duncan paused to count, "ten books?"

"Hopefully this will be enough to last the week," Hayden replied mildly.

"Why'd you come back?" Duncan demanded.

"Duncan," Birdie said.

"What?" Duncan's puzzled gaze turned to her.

"That sounded rude."

"No, it sounded curious," Duncan argued, but it didn't matter because Hayden didn't answer. Birdie wished she could get away with things like that. She felt compelled to answer any question people lobbed at her. Maybe she was a people pleaser, too. Like Sterling. Except while he had earned his angel wings trying to take care of everybody, she had earned hers trying to alternately be unobtrusive or obsequious enough to earn her father's approval. *Are we always our childhood wounds?* she wondered. Her eyes fell on Hayden. *No. Sometimes we're grownup wounds, too.*

"It didn't really matter, did it?" Duncan continued, clearly peeved by Hayden's continued silence. "You took Sterling's scholarship, went away and got a fancy degree, and still came back here with your tail between your legs."

"*Duncan,*" Birdie hissed.

"What?" Duncan snapped turning his ire on her. "Why do you sound defensive of him, Birdie? You don't know how it was."

"I know it was ten years ago," she said.

"Time's not a magic elixir to make everything better," Duncan said. "I'd think your dad would have taught you that."

Birdie drew in a sharp breath. Hayden gathered his books, tension now pouring off of him. Duncan seemed to realize the tension at the same moment and shifted into a defensive posture, as if gearing up for a fight. Vaguely, Birdie wondered if she'd be the cause of the library's first ever bare-knuckled brawl.

"I bet you still pull the wings off flies, huh, Shepherd," Hayden said. He tossed him a mocking little smirk and walked out of the library.

"Man, that guy," Duncan said, returning his attention to Birdie with an amused shrug. "What?" he asked, taking note of her livid expression.

"That was...that was so you, Duncan," she said.

He blinked at her. "What's that supposed to mean?"

"Clearly he's had a bad turn. Why would you poke at it?"

"Why would I not? You think he wouldn't do the same to me or Sterling? You think he wouldn't lord it over us if one of us wound up in dire straits?"

"No, I don't think he would. I think he wants peace and healing more than anything right now. I think he couldn't care less about petty high school rivalries."

"You *think* you know him, but you don't. And for that matter, why do you think you know anything? And why does it sound like your loyalty to him trumps your loyalty to your brother, to me?"

"Loyalty? Are you the godfather? Do I have to kiss your ring?"

He grinned at her, shifting into the new and confusing flirt mode. "Would you like to?" He leaned forward and rested on his forearms, bringing him within a hairsbreadth of her face.

"Ugh," she said, pushing her chair back to gain some distance.

"What?" he said, smiling now in what she guessed was supposed to be a seductive manner. Or at least that was the effect it had on her. She suddenly found herself wanting to forget his odious behavior and kiss him, the cad. Thus answering the question of why he'd had so many girlfriends when he was so utterly punchable. Say what she might about Duncan, and she could say a lot, but the boy had moves.

"You think you can kiss me and erase anything that's come before, that just because you make me shivery now I'll forgive all your transgressions," she said.

"It's a formula that's worked remarkably well for me these twenty-nine years," he said.

"That ends today. You cannot barge into my job, try to take over my life, be exceedingly rude to one of my…patrons, and then try to smooth it over with your lips."

He sighed, a patented my-best-friend's-little-sister-is-making-me-crazy sound. "Birdie, come on. Why you gotta be like this?"

"Different from you, you mean? With a heart and a will of my own? It's a mystery, Duncan, why I don't roll right over and let you consume me completely."

The corner of his lips twitched. "That sounds vaguely inappropriate." He pressed his face to her ear and nibbled her lobe. "I'll be sweet, I promise. Now tell me more about how I make you shivery."

"No, go away," she said, but her resolve was weakening. People probably thought she was standoffish, but really she was a deeply affectionate person, dying to touch and be touched in return. Having Duncan's lips on her felt like sensory overload. "This is why I need girlfriends," she murmured.

"For this?" he asked, lips migrating to her neck.

"No," she said, squirming away while she still had an ounce of resolve. "To talk to. To try and figure out," she waved her hand, encompassing the length of his body.

"You can talk to me. I'll help you figure it out."

"Pretty sure I know how that conversation would go," she said, tone dry.

He grinned. "I mean it though, Birdie. Come on. I've known you my whole life. What's got you so tied up in knots over this, besides the fact that you overthink absolutely everything to death, really grind it into dust, take the dead horse's bones, burn and bury them?"

"You're like my family," she said.

He gave a little nod of agreement.

"My family is complex. It brings up good and bad feelings, despite being stuck with them for life. I don't want to conflate familial belonging with romantic attachment. Does that make sense? I don't want to be with you because you're familiar and there's no one else. And I don't want you to be with me for those same reasons."

He massaged his brow. "This is what's wrong with thinking, Birdie. It complicates things that don't need to be complex. Let me simplify for you: I'm a twenty nine year old attractive male. You're a twenty six year old attractive female. We have potent chemistry. Let's put it together and see where it goes."

Eyes on him, she reached for a piece of paper from the printer, wadded it into a ball, and tossed it at him, missing by a wide margin. "Go away, with your condescension and oversimplifications of grave life matters. You annoy me greatly."

He bent, picked up the piece of paper, winged it at her, and hit the center of her forehead. "Opposites attract, and all that." Then he blew her a kiss and walked out of the library.

CHAPTER 13

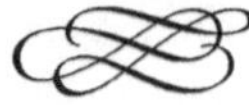

Persistence is key! Don't let discouragement stop you from being the you you want to be! Now that you've identified your goal, keep at it. DON'T LET ANYTHING STOP YOU!

I'm sorry about Duncan.

After Birdie's shift at the library, she hadn't heard from Hayden. She tossed and turned all night, thinking about the encounter at the library. Despite the fact that they were merely friends, and text-based friends at that, she couldn't help but feel guilty about Duncan. Finally, she had some adventure and romance in her life, and she had never been more confused.

Don't apologize for him.

Someone has to. Duncan has faults, I'm the first to admit that. I've been on the receiving end of a lot of them. But he is loyal, extremely so. He will always be on Sterling's side, and that means he will likely always hate you.

And now we're adding another layer to the hate cake.

Birdie laughed. *Mmm. Hate cake. Sounds delicious.*

It looks good but leaves a terrible aftertaste and heartburn, Hayden replied.

She sent him a fire emoji. He sent her a fire hose.

That felt like a rebuke, she said.

It was. Don't play with fire.

The double meaning was not lost on her. *I'm not, Hayden, honestly. That's not me. Duncan has me tied up in knots, but our relationship has not progressed beyond friendship, despite what he thinks or says. I have not given him an answer. And you...*

...And me?

You're something altogether new and different. I have no idea what to make of you and our odd arrangement. But we're friends. Tends.

Friexts.

Smiling, she set her phone aside. Then it beeped again and she picked it back up. *But also, Birdie...*

The ellipses appeared and disappeared three times before he finished.

I like you.

She didn't know how to ask him if he liked her or *liked* her liked her. There was no way to be an adult and text that question. So she said the only innocuous thing she could think of.

Same.

"I have got to get some girl friends," she muttered to herself. Somehow she thought having a girl friend would be the magic answer to all her problems, that a girl would be able to read the situation with Duncan and Hayden and provide some perspective. She had never clicked with any of the girls from her small high school, and now it felt too late to form friendships. Some of them had moved away, and the ones who hadn't were now married with babies. "I shall go to the city and find friends," she declared, rising up out of her chair with a raised fist, like Scarlet O'Hara promising to find food for her hungry brood. "As God as my witness, I will never go lonely again."

"Birdie," Shelley said, staring at her as if she'd taken leave of her senses, which she apparently had. Thankfully it was only the two of them in the office, no customers for the time being.

Birdie sat and straightened her skirt. She'd known her boss long enough that she didn't have to explain her oddity. Shelley seemed to accept it intrinsically as part of small town living, which it was. Birdie secretly believed everyone in the entire world was crazy, but in a small town you rubbed shoulders with people often enough to see behind the carefully constructed facades. Not like in a big city where you could be anonymous enough to keep your insanity on the down low. "Sorry," Birdie said.

"That's all right. It can be lonely here," Shelley said, tone sympathetic.

"Are you lonely, Shelley?" Birdie asked. Shelley was married with two teenagers, gainfully employed, and on a couple of committees in town. To Birdie, she seemed like a grand success.

"Only when I'm awake," Shelley said, tossing her a sad smile.

"But you're married," Birdie exclaimed.

Shelley laughed, albeit sadly. "Honey, marriage isn't the secret formula for lifelong happiness. You only get out of it what you bring to it. I've always been singular, had a hard time connecting with other women. That hasn't changed just because I'm middle aged now." She grimaced. "I'm middle aged now. How did that happen?" She shook her head. "Anyway, take it from someone who knows. You work on you now before you get married because after, it's a whole lot harder. You're adding another person into that mix, a person who comes with his own set of problems and expectations. Now is the prime of your life. You better enjoy it." The way she stared hard at Birdie and jutted a finger sounded ominous, like a threat.

Birdie nodded. "I will," she declared fervently. "I promise to keep Christmas in my heart, not just today, but all year long."

Shelley laughed, a real one this time. "Oh, girlie, you're a delight."

"I'm an eccentric cuckoo bird," Birdie countered, tapping her temple.

"No one said the two have to be mutually exclusive," Shelley said. Her afternoon appointment walked in, and she turned her attention to business.

That night was one of Birdie's evenings to work on her third job, the accounting one that paid the bills. Usually she set herself up in the kitchen with her computer, but there was no reason she couldn't go mobile. She loaded her computer and papers into a bag and drove forty minutes away to the next largest city.

In Georgia there was Atlanta in the north and the ocean in the south. Everything in the middle was sort of forgotten, but Birdie liked it that way, enjoyed the feeling of anonymity it gave her. It was like she had found a place to hide from the rest of the world. Absolutely no one in the world cared what happened in Little Neck, Georgia. But when she wanted to reach out to people, to find friends and get a good cup of coffee, it required driving a long distance to a town someone in the world did care about.

She reached the trendy coffee shop and set up camp at one of the booths, spreading her computer and papers wide. Innocuous background music made her feel young and trendy. *Look at me, living life to the fullest.* She picked up her coffee and took a sip, decaf because while she wanted to have grand adventures, she also wanted to sleep at night.

After a half hour of dedicated bookkeeping, she toggled her computer to Google and typed. *How to make friends.*

As ever, Google provided a bevy of suggestions. *Be approachable.* Birdie pasted on a smile. *Be interesting.* Hmm, not much she could do about that, unless by "interesting" they secretly meant "weird." *Ask others questions about themselves.* Did Birdie do that, or was she self-involved? She pulled out her phone and texted Hayden.

How are you?

Better than I've been all day. How are you?

How was she? *Trying hard to be better.*

Why? You seem amazing as is.

It was, hands down, the first time anyone in her life ever used "amazing" as a descriptor, and she was including her mother in that. *What are you up to tonight?*

Reading. What about you?

Secret 3rd job, the one I keep hidden so no one realizes how cool and exciting my life is.

You're adorable.

Awkward and confused, she texted him the first emoji that came up on her phone, a potato.

No, I mean it. You look adorable. I love when you pile your hair like that.

Her head snapped up. Hayden stood leaning against the counter with one hip. He waved. She waved in return, cheeks flushing. His head bowed over his phone and he texted.

Total coincidence, I assure you. I'm not at the stalking stage. Yet.

We must have the same taste in overpriced coffee, she returned. She glanced up, saw him watching her, and glanced back down again. *Come over?*

In answer, he walked over and sat in the booth beside her, nudging her slightly aside. She pulled her computer closer to make room for him. He withdrew a book, the third in the series she'd recommended. He commenced reading while she returned to her work.

An hour later, she finished and closed her computer, resting her head tiredly on the booth seat behind her. Hayden took her hand and laced their fingers together, giving her a squeeze, as if it were a normal part of their world to do so. Birdie rested her head on his shoulder, trying to pretend it wasn't as momentous as it felt. He kissed the top of her head. She read over his shoulder a while, and then the coffee shop closed.

He stood aside while she gathered her things and walked her to her car, opening the door for her and holding it as she slid inside. He closed the door and thumped the window. She drove away and chanced a glance in her rearview. Hayden remained in place, watching until she was well out of sight.

CHAPTER 14

Sometimes it's easy to lose sight of the you you want to be. Take heart! All
new things take practice.

"Have I lost sight of my *you you*?" Birdie asked herself, studying her reflection in the mirror.

"Why you talkin' to yourself?"

"Oh, sweet potato pie," Birdie said, hand on her chest as she whirled to see Duncan filling up her doorway. "Don't you ever knock? Or text? Or say a polite 'ahem' to announce your arrival?" She regarded his shoes, checking to see if he'd sneakily removed the treads. How else to explain his total silence while skulking?

"Ahem, I'm here," he said and knocked on the jamb he was already resting against. "Where'd you go last night? I stopped by."

"I was working," she said.

"I know, but you usually do it from home."

She quirked an eyebrow at him.

"That's right, Birdie, I know things." He tapped his temple. "I've known you for twenty six years and been keeping an eye on you for all of them. Pardon me for tracking your whereabouts."

"Now *that* sounds vaguely inappropriate. You leave my whereabouts out of this," she said, wagging a finger at him. He captured her finger and kept it, hooking their index fingers together.

"We're going to the gym tonight," he declared.

"No, we're not," she stubbornly returned.

"You're only saying that 'cause I didn't ask you all sweet."

"You've got me; I like to be asked nicely instead of told to show up places. I'm needy that way."

"You're needy in all the ways and I don't know why I'm pursuing you," he said, leaning forward to brush his lips over hers, "but as it happens, I'm doing this for Sterling."

"You're kissing me for Sterling's sake?" she asked, slightly breathless as he eased his free hand under her hair and slid his thumb along her neck.

"No, that's for my sake. We're going to the gym tonight for Sterling. He needs to get out, and if you go he'll go."

"Fine, but I'm driving myself."

"Why, when I'm already here?" he said, nibbling her earlobe. Did he do that on purpose to short circuit her ability to think clearly? Undoubtedly.

"Because you're handling me," she said.

"I'm trying my best," he said, hands easing onto her hips and tugging her closer.

"See? That. Stop it." She pushed his arms away. "You are acting like we're a foregone conclusion, and we are not."

He rolled his eyes. "Birdie, come on. I already told you I ran all the analytics. It's a match. Put us into any algorithm, and we'll come out on top. The only unknown in the scenario was the chemistry, if we could get over our lifelong acquaintance and see each other that way. And we do. Don't we?" He tipped his head to catch her eye when she tried to evade him.

"Yes, but..." she stopped talking when he captured her face and kissed her, long and slow and deep. She found herself tilting toward him, both physically and otherwise. Would it be so bad to be with Duncan? They had quite a history together. He had his faults, but she'd known him so long they were all bookmarked. And the chemistry was palpable.

Her phone buzzed, and she jolted away. "Stop, this is what I'm talking about. I know you, Duncan, I know how you operate. You're persistent and forceful, you ooze in and take over all available space. In your mind it's a foregone conclusion that we're going to try this, but I don't work that way. I need space and time, I need to think this through and make sure it's the right thing. You have to respect that." She smoothed his lapels to try and soften her delivery. Duncan was a salesman, naturally, and dressed the part, with button down shirts and ties. She liked that about him. He drove her crazy ninety percent of the time, but there were things she liked. Were they enough to make her toe over the line of demarcation between them? She had no idea. Hayden's presence had clouded the picture, complicating it further.

"Maybe all that's true, but I know you, too, Birdie. You think so much you talk yourself out of things. You're terrified to take a chance because it might be the wrong decision. Sometimes you have to leap before you look."

"Maybe so, but not when there are so many people I care about on the line."

"You and I and Sterling are grownups. We'll be fine. We've been over this." His tone was predictably impatient.

"There are more than the three of us involved."

"Who?" he asked, grinning. "Your Mom? She loves me. Your dad? He'd be thrilled."

That was undoubtedly true, at least about her father. "You'd definitely elevate my status there," she said.

He ignored the bitterness in her tone and reached for her. She put her hand on his chest. "Confound you and your busy fingers. You have to stop touching me until I come to a decision."

"But I like touching you. And now that I've started, I can't seem to stop. And it's not because I'm trying to convince you of my point of view. It's because it feels good and I like it. A lot. Maybe the most ever."

Her lashes fluttered. "Well, that was more honesty than I was prepared for. Let me put it like this. You believe the physical connection was the last question that needed answered. We've ascertained this part of things works for us and works well," she pointed between them. He grinned and wagged his brows. "But that wasn't ever my primary concern."

His brow lowered. "What are you saying here?"

"I'm saying I always found you attractive. You're stupid handsome. Emphasis on the stupid."

Now his brows touched his hairline. "You've always had a crush on me?"

"Oh, boy, it's like you're hearing through some sort of cocky filter or something." She settled her hands on his shoulders and gave him a little shake. "You're indisputably nice looking, but I don't care. I've never cared. I've seen you in every iteration possible, up to and including naked, thank you very much, broken bathroom lock. And it hasn't ever affected me a whit. What I care about, what I've always cared about, is the other ways we connect and, given our history, I'm not sure we do."

His brow furrowed, now in frustration. "Wait, if I'm hearing you properly, you're saying you might not actually be attracted to me."

"Shocking, isn't it," she said, tone dry.

"But why? What is so bad about me?"

He looked vulnerable, and she couldn't stand it. She hugged him, resting her arms on his shoulders. "Nothing. There's a lot of wonderful about you, a lot of things I love. But the world's not black and white that way. It's not good people and bad people, people you love and people you can't stand. I'm trying to tell you I don't know. I don't know if I see you as more than my brother's annoying best friend because I've never tried before. I need time and space to think it through, to figure it out."

He blew out a breath, frowning. "And what am I supposed to be doing while you do that?"

"You're supposed to back off and let me."

"I'm not good at backing off," he conceded, fiddling with the last button on her untucked shirt.

"That's what made you Central Georgia's top regional salesman, three years running," she said, resting her head on his shoulder as she hugged him again. Smiling now, he returned her hug, resting his head on hers. It was nice, a sweet moment of peace after what felt like a long and stormy few decades of conflict. He rubbed a comforting little circle on her back, then reached down and pinched her butt, hard.

"Get dressed, Chickie. I'll meet you at the gym." Standing, he patted her head and walked out of her room, laughing as Birdie picked up her slipper and winged it at him, missing by a mile.

CHAPTER 15

Thinks he knows me, does he? Birdie stood and rifled her closet, searching for the fancy workout clothes she'd purchased but never had the nerve to wear. She found them, a matching set of spandex pants and midriff-bearing tank top. Usually she wore a pair of jogging pants and one of Sterling's old castoff t-shirts to work out, but she was trying to get her *you you* in order. Time to mix things up. The store-bought outfit was not only form fitting and revealing, the shirt was also neon pink, a color Birdie was certain she'd never worn in her life. If she ever wore pink, which she rarely did, it was always a soft shell color. As she put on the clothes and inspected herself in the mirror, she wondered why.

"I think pink is my color," she whispered. Her hair and eyes were dark brown, meaning her skin was light with natural pink undertones. The pink of the shirt made everything pop, unlike the earth tones she usually wore. Why did she dress like background noise, if it wasn't what she wanted to be? *Time for some color,* she promised herself. She piled her hair on top of her head and clipped it in place, laying her own odds on how long it would remain. Her hair seemed to have a stubborn streak that considered all authority in need of rebellion. *Try to contain me, I dare you,* she could almost hear it say. Maybe she should take a few pointers from her tresses.

She curled her lashes, applied some mascara, and reached for her gloss, the pink stuff she hadn't worn since she was a kid, back when she tried to make herself more apparent.

It's ridiculous to make yourself up to go to the gym, her brain insisted.

Ask me if I care, she returned, pointing her gloss menacingly at the mirror. *Listening to you hasn't taken me very far in life, brain. Your time is over. My you you and I are taking chances now.* She dropped the gloss in her purse, grabbed a bottle of water, and darted out the door.

Her defiant determination lasted exactly until she reached the gym and then she was stuck, tight fisting the steering wheel. What had she been thinking? She couldn't go to the gym with an exposed midriff like some kind of girl who, who...went to the gym with an exposed midriff. On the other hand, it was only Sterling and Duncan. Even if Duncan had never returned the favor and accidentally peeped her naked, he'd seen her just about every other way—in her swimsuit, pajamas, first thing in the morning. Not a lot of surprises left between them. Plus, the car was hot enough to make her perish. That more than anything compelled her from it.

Sterling and Duncan were already there. She noted their cars, aiming for nonchalance as she pulled open the door and stepped inside. Sterling sat on the weight bench, staring at his phone, face unshaved, looking uncharacteristically miserable. Duncan glanced up, did a double take, and froze, mouth agape as his eyes scraped over her. His gaze darted to Sterling and found him still oblivious. He pointed to Birdie and gave her a thumb's up and mouthed, *Hot.* She pointed to him, tight t-shirt stretched across ridiculously defined chest and abs, and tilted her flattened hand back and forth. *Meh, you'll do.* He rolled his eyes, but he was grinning. Birdie headed toward the elliptical, thought better of it, diverted to Sterling, and gave him a swallowing hug.

"What's up?" she said. She hadn't seen him in days, and she missed him terribly.

Far from being annoyed by the hug, as he usually might have been, he briefly rested his head on her shoulder and closed his eyes. "Hey. Nothin'. What's up with you?"

"She's lookin' all hot to trot, that's what's up," Duncan said.

Sterling finally opened his eyes and looked at her, grimacing as he took in her outfit. "What on earth, Birdie? Why are you trying to look like a girl in front of Duncan? You know he's susceptible."

"The combined misogyny in this gym is enough to reset the women's movement to before the 19th Amendment," Birdie said.

"What does our sexism have to do with slavery?" Duncan asked.

"That's the 13th Amendment, you muscle-headed dimwit. Pick up a book now and again," Birdie replied.

"Maybe I know and I'm teasing you to get a reaction," he replied.

"You don't know," she said.

"Nah, I don't know," he agreed, unconcerned. "We doing this, or what?" he added to Sterling who was once again ignoring them in favor of his phone. Birdie edged away from them, toward her BFF, the elliptical. She started to glide. The door opened, and she didn't have to look to know it was Hayden. Somehow their lives were synching up without either of them trying.

He took the treadmill beside her elliptical and started to run at a moderate pace. They exercised in easy silence a while. Birdie congratulated herself that the workouts were coming easier, the post-elliptical recovery less painful and exhausting. And, if she were being honest, she would never admit how much she enjoyed it. There was something to be said for those post-workout endorphins. Her body hummed with energy and good cheer, even if everything else in her life was currently a mess.

Duncan appeared suddenly before her. "Bah," she yelped, reaching out a hand to avoid tumbling off the machine.

Grinning, he knocked on the elliptical. "Ahem, I'm here."

"Excellent. Now go away. I'm in a zone here."

"The slow ambler's zone?" he said. "My grandma does this faster."

"Set up a race. I guarantee I'll take her," Birdie replied. Beside them, Hayden snickered. Duncan tossed him a scowl and angled his body, trying to exclude him from hearing, even though he was a mere two feet away.

"Come lift weights."

"Why?"

"Because I said so."

"It's fun how you keep the dream alive that ordering me to do something will work just once in our lives," she said.

"Lifting weights is important," he said, tone longsuffering.

"Important to whom?"

"To people who use the gym and don't say whom," he replied, reaching forward to turn up her machine.

"I'm pacing myself so I don't turn into a muscle-bound she-woman," Birdie replied, turning down her machine, and Hayden snickered again.

"Birdie, I swear. Get over to the weight bench."

"That's another example of telling, not asking," she told him.

He glanced away and lowered his voice. "I need some help with Sterling. He's not responding." His throat bobbed as he swallowed reflexively.

"Well, that's a horse of a different color," Birdie said and turned off her machine. She followed Duncan to the weight machine.

"I brought Birdie," he announced loudly to Sterling as if they were visitors to the old folks' home. "Let's set her up with some weights. What do you think we should start with?"

"This looks good," Birdie said, picking up a small one.

"That's the stopper for the end of the bar, dummy," Duncan said, taking it out of her fingers.

"And yet I already feel more developed," Birdie said, poking her lackluster bicep.

"No, you don't," Duncan said, giving the same bicep a squeeze as his thumb made a sneaky and soothing little pass over the tender inside of her arm.

"Nothing too big," Birdie said sincerely because Duncan had a habit of trying to push her beyond her means. In every facet of life, apparently.

"Don't be such a softie. Lie down."

She crossed her arms over her chest, rooted to the spot. He hissed a breath through his teeth.

"Birdie, would you pretty please lie on the weight bench so we may help you with your physical fitness?"

"Was that so hard?" she replied, easing forward to straddle the bench and lie down.

"I swear," Duncan muttered, reaching for the bar. Her eyes skittered to Hayden. He appeared to be intent on his workout, but the tense set of his shoulders told Birdie he was eavesdropping on them. His face was pinched, and she wondered why, suddenly remembering she had a text she ignored. Was that why? Had she hurt his feelings with her lack of response? She sat up. Duncan pushed her back down. "I'll tie you if I have to."

"I need my phone."

"Nice try. Besides, there's enough of that going around." Both of them looked at Sterling who ignored them in equal measure. "Now, I started you small because, you being a wimp, I'd expect nothing less. These are nice ten pounders." He thumped the weight on one end of the bar. She put her hands up, then drew them back down again.

"Doesn't the bar weigh something?"

He rolled his eyes. "Hardly anything. Yeesh, Chickie, you are a coward in all the ways today. Put your hands on the bar and pick it up."

"So motivational," Birdie groused, but she put her hands on the bar and gave it a shove. *I'm dying,* she thought as the full measure of the bar's weight hit her. She brought it to her chest and, with shaking Jell-O arms, lifted it back up again.

"That's good, keep it going," Duncan encouraged.

"No," she grunted. "Take it."

He shook his head. She remained frozen, bar extended perilously overhead. She understood he wouldn't actually let it drop on her, but she also understood he believed she could do this. And she couldn't. Her arms felt like her muscles were tearing into shreds. Tears sprang to her eyes, but she would not, could not cry in front of Duncan who already thought she was a weakling. There was nothing for it but to power through until he'd decided she had enough.

And then suddenly the bar was gone, back in its rack. "The bar weighs forty five pounds. Sixty-five pounds is too much for a beginner. Can't you see she's in pain?" Hayden said, standing beside her, his presence an angry tower.

"She's stronger than she looks, and I know what I'm doing," Duncan said, an equally angry tower on her other side.

"Stop trying to make her who you want her to be instead of appreciating her as she is," Hayden replied.

Duncan expelled a grunt of either humor or exasperation. "What on earth do you know about it? This is so like you, Paxton. Inserting your nose where it doesn't belong."

"And this is so like you, Shepherd, trampling a hapless woman for the sake of your own vanity," Hayden said.

Birdie tried to sit up, but Sterling preempted her in a tired tone. "Y'all stop. Duncan, the bar was too much. Paxton, this really isn't your concern."

"If you don't want me to insert myself, then set down your phone and take better care of her," Hayden said. Not waiting for a response, he turned and stormed from the gym.

"Man, that guy," Duncan muttered. "You're fine, aren't you, Birdie?" He glanced down at her, uncertainty marring his handsome features.

"I don't know," she said slowly. Her muscles were still aquiver, but, more than that, the scene had been confusing. Birdie had always counted Sterling as her number one protector, and Duncan secondary to that. If she'd been the kind of girl to find herself in trouble, she always knew she could call Duncan if Sterling wasn't available and he would come to her aid, no questions asked. But tonight it had been Hayden to step in and provide help. And what was more confusing was how natural it had felt.

Sterling helped her sit up while Duncan fidgeted, re-racking the weights. He hated to be wrong, even more than he hated to have anyone point out his wrongness. She shook out her arms. "I'm fine," she assured them.

"Of course you are," Duncan said, relieved. She reached for her purse, arms still trembly, and fished for her phone, swiping it to read her last text from Hayden, the one she'd missed.

Today would have been my anniversary.

"Oh, man, I've gotta go," she said, darting to her feet. Neither of the men responded. Skirting by them without a goodbye, she dodged outside and leaned on her car, texting a fast and furious reply.

I'm so sorry, I just saw this. What a miserable, crummy event for you. How can I help? What can I do?

Nothing. It is what it is. Are you okay?

Yep. Thanks for the rescue. I might hate the gym.

Hate the player, not the game, he replied.

Maybe I'll hate both. What are you doing now?

Staring into the abyss, contemplating the futility of life. Same old, same old.

Are you living with your dad?

Nope, got my own place.

Address, please, she requested.

He gave it and then, *Why? What's your plan?*

She didn't reply. She couldn't because she was too busy flitting to the store, gathering a care package. She put in a carton of ice cream, a box of tissues, a stress ball, a stuffed bunny, and a Nicholas Sparks book. It wasn't great, but it was the quickest thing she could assemble last minute. She arranged her purchases in the little basket, then set it on his doorstep, rang the bell, and dodged around the corner.

He opened the door, his head peering back and forth as if looking for her. Then he noted the basket. He knelt and retrieved it, smiling as he sifted through it.

This is great, he texted. *Although I have to admit I was hoping for something else, a bit more personal, perhaps.* He stepped inside and closed the door. Birdie dithered in her hiding spot around the corner.

"I am brave," she whispered to herself and reached for her phone. *Come back out.*

A few seconds later, he opened the door and poked his head out. Birdie sprinted onto the porch and pelted herself at him, leaping as she wrapped her arms and legs around him in a swallowing koala hug. He returned her hug, squeezing impossibly tight, head pressed to her shoulder. Her hand made a few soothing passes over his head. She kissed his cheek. He gave her one final squeeze and set her down. She back-stepped to her car, keeping her eyes on him, then got in and drove away.

A minute later her phone beeped with a text.

In case I forget to tell you, pink is my new favorite color.

She smiled, tossing her phone in her purse. *Mine, too,* she thought. From now on, she promised to do her best not to hide anymore.

CHAPTER 16

*H*er mom was at the kitchen table when she arrived home, nursing a glass of sweet tea. When Birdie was a kid, sweet tea had been as ubiquitous as their native peaches, but like everything else good it couldn't last. Sugar was on the list of no-no foods now, meaning they only made sweet tea for special occasions. Her mom must have had a rough day if she was drinking it now.

"What's up?" Birdie asked, taking the seat beside her.

"Nothing, just work stress. Being a stay at home mom has a lot of upsides when you have to deal with humanity on a daily basis. Maybe you could have babies and I could reclaim my glory days by watching them fulltime."

"Well, that's a lot to unpack for a weeknight," Birdie declared.

Her mother laughed and took another sip of tea. "Duncan's been around a lot lately. Haven't seen him here so much since Sterling moved out."

"He's like a human case of the hives. He turns up when it's least convenient," Birdie hedged.

"Y'all dating?"

"Give me a sip of that tea, Mom, so I can comically spurt it all over the table," Birdie said, holding out her hand. Her mother obligingly handed her the tea, but Birdie drank it, enjoying the soothing luxury of chilled syrup sliding down her throat. Comfort in a glass, that's what it was.

"Stall tactics," her mom noted. "I'm well versed."

"I learned from the master. The truth is I don't know. Maybe. He wants to. Why, though?"

"You need a motherly pep talk about all your finer points?"

"No. Well, maybe at some point, but not now. I meant what on earth made him flip a switch and set his sights on me? It's like it's the year 1984 and Arnold Schwarzenegger has selected me for termination."

Her mom laughed. "Duncan likes two things: quality and familiarity. You have both of those in spades."

"I'm not certain that's enough."

"I'd think long and hard about it."

That surprised her. "You don't like me and Duncan together? I thought you'd be overjoyed not to have to get used to someone new and unknown."

"First of all, it's not about me and my comfort level. Second, I love Duncan. He's like a third kid. But I'm not oblivious to his faults. The two of you have always been like oil and water."

"He seems to think that's indicative of good chemistry," Birdie mused.

"Maybe. Or maybe you simply annoy the ever-loving stuffing out of each other."

"How do you know?" Birdie asked.

Her mother shrugged.

"How did you know? With Dad, how did you know you wanted to marry him?"

Her mother blew out a breath. "Because I loved him. Because he could be charming and attentive and funny. Because I was too young and naïve to heed the warning signs. Because I didn't yet understand the heavy toll mental illness can take on a marriage."

"And if you'd known, if you'd heeded the signs, would you still have done it?"

"I don't know, Birdie. You and Sterling are worth anything, you know that. Every moment of my marriage was worth it to get you two. But, excluding you, if you're asking if I'd do it all over again, I honestly don't know. You can't possibly understand the toll it takes on you to be in a bad marriage like that, mentally, emotionally, physically, financially. For the last decade your dad and I were together, every moment of every day was defined by his moods."

"And yet he was the one who left," Birdie said.

Her mom sighed. "Because, much like you, once I love, I love for life. I'd probably still be with your dad, if he hadn't walked away. That's how we're built, you and I. We hold people at arm's length, but then once they're in, they're always in. So take heed, daughter, that you don't fall in love lightly. Because once you do, it will be forever."

Birdie shuddered. "Knowing how horribly it could turn out, why would I ever want to?"

"Because, bad as it was, there were still good moments. At night, for instance, we'd lie in bed and I'd shuffle next to him. He's slip his arm over my waist, and for those few moments, everything was okay. We were connected. All the bad stuff didn't matter. I was safe, I was loved. We had each other. The good moments, when everything worked and we were really man and wife, that's what I strove for, why I never gave up. Because when it was good, it was amazing."

"But when it was bad, it was horrible," Birdie said.

Her mom nodded.

"I'm worried about Sterling," Birdie blurted.

"Sterling's fine," her mom declared. Birdie caught the hint of desperation in her voice and understood what she was actually saying. *I need Sterling to be fine.* In a volatile family, Sterling had become their anchor. Her mother needed Sterling to remain so to keep her own world in balance. A few weeks ago, Birdie might have felt the same, but now it was as if the blinders had been pulled off and she could see the toll playing the family gatekeeper had taken on her brother.

But what could she do about it? Tell her mother not to call him when she had car trouble or house trouble or had a financial question? Her mom had no one else. She had transferred everything she used to get from their dad to him, and the weight of it was too much. On the other hand, it wasn't fair that her mom couldn't depend on him. And their dad…

Birdie sighed. She knew what she needed to do, but she didn't want to do it. Before she could find a way to talk herself out of it, she picked up her phone and texted her father.

Hey, Dad, let's have supper tomorrow. My treat.

I don't feel like going out, came the immediate reply. It would be so easy to let that be that, to say that she'd tried. But her father had a mental illness. He was depressed; of course he didn't feel like going out.

Come on, it's meatloaf night at the diner. I know that's your favorite. It'll be… What could she say? Fun? No, it wouldn't be fun. *…a good chance to catch up.* There. That was as truthful as she could currently be. She and her dad had a lot to catch up on, her entire life, for instance.

He didn't return her text for another hour, but that was nothing unusual. Eventually he replied.

Okay. Meet you there at six.

She set her phone aside with a smile. She was taking life by the horns, even her dad. Things could only go up from here, right? The answer, as it turned out, was a definitive no.

CHAPTER 17

he next day at lunch, Birdie went to see her brother. She had purposely stayed away for days, and now it was time to check in. But when she put her hand on the door of his store, she found it locked. Knocking, she pressed her face to the door. Everything was dark. She pulled out her phone and sent him a text.

AT YOUR STORE. *What's up?*

HE TEXTED A MINUTE LATER. *Had a thing, no biggie.*

YOU OKAY? *Need anything?*

I'M FINE, *thanks.*

. . .

HER HAND HOVERED over her phone, pondering. Should she tell him about her dinner with their father that night and invite him along? No doubt she wanted him there as a buffer. She couldn't remember a time she'd had a meal alone with her father without Sterling running interference. But she was a grownup, and it was time to take the pressure off Sterling. Surely she could survive one meal without her big brother there to protect her.

She passed Hayden's store and paused to look inside. He stood behind the desk, working on something. He glanced up at her, tossing her a warm smile. She touched her fingers to her eyes and pointed them at him. He did the same gesture in return. She waved. He waved, and she continued on her way. A second later, her phone buzzed with his text.

STATUS REPORT, *and go:*

STATUS REPORT, hmm. What was her status today? She felt...optimistic. Life was changing somehow, in some indefinable way. And so far she was happy with those changes.

EVERYTHING'S COMING UP ROSES. You?

MY WIFE TEXTED LAST NIGHT.

BIRDIE SANK INTO HER CHAIR. *I had to sit down for that one. What did she want?*

TO WISH ME A HAPPY ANNIVERSARY.

. . .

FOR REAL?

YES. It was kind of nice, actually, like some sign things affected her, at least a little. She moved on so easily. That was the part I couldn't understand. Did our time together mean nothing to her? Was our marriage a lie? Was I that replaceable?

EASY QUESTION: no. You are not easily replaceable, Hayden Paxton. Do you think she's having regrets?

MAYBE SOME, at least about the way it went down, the hurt it caused.

Do you think she wants to get back together?

DUNNO.

WOULD YOU WANT TO, if she did?

THE RIGHT ANSWER is to say no, of course not. She destroyed me, took away my trust, my job, my best friend. Of course I wouldn't want to get back together with that. Who in his right mind would?

WHAT'S THE REAL ANSWER, she prompted.

I REALLY DON'T KNOW, Birdie. When I love, I love deep. It felt like an amputation when our marriage ended. But if things resumed, would it go back to feeling how it was, or would it feel like someone tried to use school glue to patch the missing limb back on?

Is she still with the guy? The ex-best?

To my knowledge, yes. And the real clincher? I miss him, too. What is wrong with me?

Nothing. You said it already; you love deep. Maybe instead of regaining what was lost, you need to work on finding absolution in the way that suits you best, on letting go of the anger and hurt while retaining the positive emotions. Believe me when I tell you it's possible to love someone and still guard your heart. It's possible to give needed grace without reducing yourself to rubble.

Something to ponder, wise one. Thanks for letting me spew.

Spew Handler, that's me.

Spew Manager. You were due for a promotion, he said.

There'd better be a pay increase, she warned.

Double hugs, he said.

I'll take it.

. . .

THE ELLIPSES APPEARED a few times before he texted again. *Is it too weird to tell you all this?*

No, absolutely no. We. Are. Friends.

Emphatic.

Yes. I. Am. And we're honest. It's sort of our thing. Hayden and Birdie: they were always honest with each other. That's what it will say on our tombstones. I ordered adjoining ones. Don't freak out.

No, it was definitely time. I was ready for the next step. Adjoining tombstones was definitely it. Quick question: where do we go from here?

THE QUESTION FELT HALF-SERIOUS. No way would Birdie respond to it, not after he'd just poured his heart out over his ex-wife. *Matching toothbrushes, obviously. It's like you've never been tends with a woman before.*

Friexts. And you're definitely my first.

LATER, when she went to her car at the end of the day, she opened the door and saw a brand new toothbrush, still in its package, lying on her front seat. A moment later Hayden sent her a text of the same toothbrush in his hand. *Done and done.*

. . .

Now it's getting serious, she replied.

FINALLY, he returned.

SHE WAS STILL SMILING when she entered the diner that night, at least until she saw her dad sitting at a table, alone and hunched. He looked so sad, so defeated, so *alone.* Not for the first time Birdie wished she could help him, fix whatever was wrong in his brain to make him the way he was.

"Hey, Dad," she said, aiming for a breezy tone as she sank into the chair across from him. "What's shaking?" She said it flippantly, but she meant it earnestly. What was going on in her father's life? She had no idea. She hadn't known even when she was a kid, before he walked out on their family.

He gave a little shrug. "Where's Sterling?"

"Your guess is as good as mine. He's elusive lately."

"Probably with the girlfriend," he said.

"Do you like Chelsea?"

"I think he could do better."

"That's where we agree. But, really, who could possibly be good enough for Sterling? It's like you and Mom knew when you named him how good he'd turn out."

He smiled a little. The way to his heart was always to talk about the chosen one. With a pang, she wondered if he'd ever once looked liked that when someone mentioned her name, such a mixture of pride and fondness. The waitress came to take their order. With the menus gone, they were left with nothing to do with their hands, no way to hide their faces. It was more like being on a bad first date than with her biological father of twenty six years.

"How's your mother?" he asked after a moment of awkward silence. It wasn't so much that Birdie didn't know how to make small talk, but rather she hated the fact that she had to resort to small talk with her father.

"She's good. Work's been a little stressful, but you know," she shrugged as if to say, *what are you going to do?*

He huffed a sigh. "She shouldn't have taken so much time off work. It made her unemployable."

"I thought you and Mom both wanted her to stay home with us," Birdie said.

"No, that was all your mother. We could have done so much better financially, if she had worked all those years."

Birdie thought of those years, of how her mother had always been there, no matter what. When her father raged or stayed in his room for weeks on end, her mother had picked up the slack, went to every one of her piano recitals or Sterling's games, packed their lunches, was the room mother for both of them, made certain they had clean laundry, listened to their problems, helped them with their homework. What would their life have been like if she had been at work all those many evenings when their father was locked in his room, yelling at imaginary demons and throwing things or, worse, weeping? What would have become of them if she and Sterling had been left to their own devices all those years, if they hadn't had that one solid, unshakeable parent to depend on? And, while she was on the topic, the money problems had been his fault, no question. He was the one who bought new cars, a piano, a pool table, an actual pool, and anything else he deemed a necessity during his manic impulse phases. One year, a month before Christmas, he invested their entire savings in a startup herbal drink company that went belly up three weeks later. Christmas had been nonexistent that year, saved only by the traditions her mother insisted on carrying out—cookies, cocoa, and all the other rituals that soothed them during their painful, unruly childhood.

"Hmm," Birdie said, stuffing aside the old wounds. It would do no good, absolutely no good to argue. Might, in fact, make everything worse.

"Is she dating anyone?"

Despite the fact that he had been the one to walk out and demand a divorce, he remained incurably jealous over his ex-wife. Birdie opened her mouth to blurt that of course her mother wasn't dating anyone, but closed it instead. "That's probably a better question for her. It's not like moms talk to their daughters about their dating lives, you know?"

He frowned. "Yes, but, wouldn't you know?"

"With Mom? Are you joking? You know how private she is." That part was true. Her mother was the type of woman who would carry on a serious romance, get married, and only tell someone on her deathbed when it came time to change the will. "Are you seeing anyone, Dad?" Like Sterling, her father was a nice looking man, not averse to female attention. He had dated a few random women over the years, but all of them bugged out at the first sign of trouble, which was to say none of them lasted longer than a couple of weeks.

"I've been talking to a few women on the internet. Not much going on here, you know?" He motioned to the diner around them.

"Please don't give any of them money," Birdie said.

"Oh, Birdie," he said, shaking his head. She noticed he didn't say he wouldn't. Her father was prime pickings for being catfished, getting caught up in a sob story and giving all his money away.

Their food arrived. They spent some time eating in silence. *Ask me about me, about my life,* she silently pled. When she was in school, he routinely asked about her grades. If her memory served, that was the last relevant question he ever asked her. For a brief flicker, she was tempted to tell him she was considering dating Duncan. It would, she knew, be the gateway to his approval. Duncan was the sort of man her father could sink his teeth into—handsome, brawny, a former football star like Sterling, financially successful by their small town standards. But not only would she never use Duncan that way, she couldn't give her father false hope if it didn't work out. Not least of which because he would never let it go. And then if she did date Duncan and things didn't work out, her father would blame Birdie for the failure, regardless of who was at fault. She was preemptively exhausted from carrying out a conversation in her head, so much that she didn't at first notice the way her father tensed and stared toward the door.

She turned to look and saw Hayden and *his* father enter. They paused, talking to people along the way. His father was a fixture in town, as beloved and stable as her father wasn't. He'd been the town handyman for decades, warm, friendly, kind. He was like a younger, skinnier, Santa. It had been a blow to everybody when he had a massive stroke. Birdie saw the signs of it now, in the way his foot dragged a pace behind the other, in the arm that hung limply at his side, at the mouth, permanently drawn on one side while the other quirked upward. It was a newly lopsided smile that only increased his cheerful looking demeanor.

Hayden stood patiently behind him, nodding at everyone his father talked to, occasionally adding a word when his chatty parent allowed. He caught sight of Birdie, did a double take, and gave her a warmer, more sincere smile she returned.

"That Paxton boy," her father muttered.

"Dad, please," Birdie hissed. The diner was small, plenty small enough for others to overhear.

"What? I have to pretend it doesn't bother me to see him strutting around town, flaunting?"

"He's not flaunting anything," Birdie said.

Her dad humphed. "Of course he is. Taking up residence right beside your brother. You tell me how that's not flaunting."

"Dad, his store was there first," she said in a tiny whisper, hoping he would lower his voice. When her dad got worked up, he tended toward sonic boom. And he was definitely getting worked up now.

"It makes me sick to think of it, what your brother could have been if he'd gotten that scholarship."

"Dad, please."

The diner was tiny, not allowing space for feuds, meaning the waitress sat Hayden and his father at a table nearby.

"Stuck as a bookseller in our tiny town. He could have gotten out, gone away, made something of himself. Not like me, tied down here with a wife and kids."

Inwardly, Birdie winced. Perhaps he was all purged now and would move on. "Can we talk about something else?"

Ignoring her, his eyes landed murderously on Hayden and his

father. She could tell by their tense demeanor and hunched shoulders they'd heard every word.

"If I had a son like that, I'd be ashamed. Probably why Harry had a stroke," her dad declared and then looked at Birdie when she smacked the table between them.

"That is enough. How could you say something so incredibly horrible and insensitive and most of all untrue? Over a silly high school feud?"

"Silly? This was your brother's big chance."

"Sterling hated football, Dad. If you had ever once thought of anyone but yourself and your needs and your feelings, you would have realized that. Did you ever think it was odd your super athlete son chose a career selling books? Do you really think I'm the only geek in our family? He was so relieved when that scholarship passed him by. Let it go. And while I know spending an evening having dinner with the person you like least, your daughter, might be a burden, that is no excuse to say something so heartless about someone who has never been anything but kind and good, not only to our family, but to everyone in this community."

"For goodness sake, Birdie, calm down. You're making a scene. My lands, you are exactly like your mother."

Hands shaking, she picked up her purse and began digging for her wallet. "Well, thank the good Lord for that small mercy," she said as she withdrew enough bills to cover supper and a tip, tossed them on the table, and fled the restaurant.

She closed herself in her car, cranked the air conditioning, and pulled out her phone. Hands shaking, she started to type a text.

I'M SO SORR...

THERE WAS a light tap on the window. She glanced up to see Hayden standing at the passenger side. He opened the door and sat down. Her face must be puce with mortification, misery, and repressed tears. She opened her mouth. He touched his finger gently to it.

"Shh, shh, shh," he said softly.

She pressed her hand to her eyes and burst into tears. He gathered her close and held her while she did an ugly cry against his chest. When her tears abated to sniffy little shudders, he pushed her away from him and offered up a smile. She gave a tentative one in return. He kissed each of her eyelids, eased from the car, and walked away.

CHAPTER 18

"What's wrong with you?"

Duncan sat on her couch when she returned home. She probably should have been annoyed to see him or, at the least, surprised. But she was too drained and numb to feel anything. She sank beside him and propped her feet on the coffee table.

"Dinner with my dad."

"Ah." He slumped, resting his feet on the table beside hers.

She wondered, suddenly, what Duncan would have done if he had been there. Would he have remained silent? Heaped more hate on Hayden? In the past he seemed to bask in the runoff of adulation from Sterling, lapping up all the leftovers her father had to extol. Back in the day, when their family had been intact, there had been plenty of it to go around. Her dad used to love to re-do a play-by-play of their games, a virtual highlight reel of the best moves, the times they were cheated. Birdie and her mother had sat by, trading glances and shrugs. Occasionally her mother or Sterling would try to work in something about Birdie—a good grade, a much-praised essay. Her father would toss her a nod in acknowledgement and redirect to his forgone favorite, the golden one.

"What?" Duncan asked, and she realized she was staring at him.

"What do you think of my dad?"

"Honestly?" He reached out and twirled his fingers in the curls lying on her collarbone. "I think he's a whack job and it's only by some miracle you and Sterling have turned out so well."

"You always seemed to like him."

"Never said I didn't like him. I can feel more than one way about a person," he replied. "A better question would be how do you feel about your dad?"

"Weary, mostly. I'm so tired of trying with him. The future is stretched out in front of me like a long dusty road."

"So maybe you give up," he said.

She had been staring straight ahead, but she turned to face him again, in surprise this time. "He's family."

"He hurts you," he said softly, pressing a tender kiss to her temple.

"I didn't think you cared," she said.

"Birdie, I swear," he said, then leaned in and kissed her collarbone, trailing kisses up the column of her throat to her lips, softly, sweetly. Birdie returned it, curling his shirt in her fist to keep him anchored in place. The kiss broke off and she rested her head on his shoulder. He slid his arm around her and cinched her closer, resting his head on hers. "I came to ask, nicely, if you want to go out tomorrow."

"Like on a date?"

"Yes, Birdie, like on a date."

"Can it be a real first date?" she asked.

"I intend to pay, if that's what has your feathers in a fuss."

"I meant an experiment, like two people who don't know each other and are trying to instead of two people who've known each other their whole lives jumping into the middle of something," she said.

He was quiet for a few beats, processing. "How do we do that? You want to pretend not to know each other?"

He said it sarcastically, but she sat up, suddenly enthused. "Could we? I would love that."

"You are so weird," he said.

"You're not supposed to know that yet." She poked him.

He rolled his eyes. "Fine, we'll pretend not to know each other. I swear, I did not predict the person I've known the longest would be the one to make me work the hardest."

She sat back, leaving some space between them. "What did you predict? Did you think I would fall all over myself in gratitude for your attention?"

"Maybe, a bit. I mean, when's the last time you had a date? It's not like you've got so many offers lined up, and I've hardly been without someone since…Where are you going?"

"I'm leaving before I stab you in the liver with an icepick," she said, not bothering to turn around.

"Are we still on for tomorrow?" he called, his voice following her down the hall.

"Only if you learn to mind your manners, you self-adoring, big headed turkey giblet," she yelled in reply.

When he let himself out soon after, she was pretty sure he was chuckling.

* * *

SHE ARRIVED in her room and received a text from Hayden.

Rough night.

Ugh. For the record, I'm so sorry about the things my dad said.

You have to stop apologizing for things that aren't your responsibility to be sorry for.

But I am sorry. You have no idea, I'm so sorry, she said, eyes blurring with tears again.

You have to stop apologizing because…I used to make fun of your dad back in the day. When we were in school.

That stopped her cold. *Why?*

It was the only way to get to Sterling, seemingly the only thing he was sensitive about, his one weakness. Your brother has good reason to hate me, that fact chief among them. And I'm the one who's sorry, I shouldn't have done that. If it's any consolation, I would never do that now. And not only because we're friends and I care, but because I realize the toll mental illness can take. You and Sterling are both so amazingly strong and resilient.

We have a good mom.

The text bubble disappeared and came back a few times before he texted again. *Will you forgive me for being a real jerk ten years ago?*

I didn't know you then.

Still, you were affected indirectly by my idiocy.

Yes, if you'll forgive me for the way my father's words are indirectly related to me.

You are not responsible for your father's actions, and I will never hold them against you. This. Is. My. Solemn. Vow.

Emphatic, she typed, smiling.

Yes. I. Am.

She took a deep breath and sent the next text before she could lose her nerve. *I have a date with Duncan tomorrow.*

Might be time for that grave plot you bought me.

I'm sorry. Should I be sorry? I don't know. You and I have something special, but we've never declared it anything more than friendship. And you still have an ex-wife very much in the way of being anything more.

You're right, of course you're right...I just...You're right. Sigh. This is hard. I'm not in any shape to move on right now, but if I were, I'd want it to be with you. You're free to date, even if I think you could do better.

I don't know that I want it to be anything with Duncan, but I feel like I have to try, to see where it goes. If not, I'll always wonder. Her eyes darted to the self-help manual. *I've been reading this book.*

Which one? You're my new hookup for recommendations.

You wouldn't like this one. It's a pop-psychology self-help manual, called Mend Over Matter, *totally ridiculous.*

Then why are you reading it?

Because I'm tired of being me.

Why?

Because I'm a comma.

...I feel we're usually on the same wavelength, B, but I have no idea what that means.

All my life I've felt outside of everything. My dad made it clear Sterling should have been an only child, and maybe it's a bleed over from that. Or maybe it's my natural personality. Whatever the reason, I am white noise, the tiny little divot in the sentence that absolutely no one notices.

First of all, commas serve a vital function. Let's eat Grandma. Let's eat, Grandma. See?

Ha.

Second, do you know you were the first person I noticed when I came back to town? You used to parade daily past my shop, from yours to Sterling's, and I would watch your little face lit with secret amusement. Sometimes you talk to yourself and move your lips, bet you didn't know that. Sometimes you looked downright angry, sometimes sad. You made me smile, made me come out of myself and think about something else, if only that I wanted to get to know that Birdie Thompson girl, 'cause she's as interesting as she is cute.

You know what you are? You're a set of quotation marks. You see them and sit up a little because you know something important is about to be said, and then you get to the end and see the other one and realize it's been a conversational hug. That's what you are, Hayden Paxton. A. Conversational. Hug.

Emphatic.

Yes. You. Are.

Birdie, I kind of adore you.

Hayden, same.

The next night Duncan rang the bell like an actual first date. He hadn't rung the bell since...Birdie wasn't certain he'd ever rung the bell. He was always *there*, tagging along with Sterling, hoovering up all their leftovers, sweet tea, and Cokes, stinky feet on the coffee table, obnoxious laugh obscuring the sound on the TV, sweaty discarded t-shirts tossed on the bathroom floor after a pickup game of one on one. And now he stood on her front porch with a bouquet of flowers, hair wet and curling from his shower, wearing a freshly pressed pair of khaki pants and crisp blue oxford.

"Miss Birdie," he said smoothly, handing her the flowers.

"Duncan." She blinked at the flowers. "Now how did you know peonies are my favorite?"

"Must have been a lucky guess, seeing as how we've never met before. This is my first blind date, by the way."

"I used to have them all the time, but then I got the Lasik," she said, tapping her eyes.

His cheek twitched. "You seem a bit odd. I'll chalk it up to first date jitters."

"Special, that's the word you're searching for. Let me put these in some water. Would you like to come in?" She moved aside and turned toward the kitchen. He followed her in and closed the door.

"Nice place you have here," he mused, turning in a slow circle. "Homey."

"Thank you."

"Have you lived here long?"

"All my life. It was a real pain when I was younger, mostly because of my brother and his annoying friends. But since he moved out, it's been a little slice of heaven."

"Kind of weird you still live with your mom. A red flag, if I'm being honest. Like maybe you're emotionally stunted or something."

"No worries. I'd have to have a heart to begin with to be emotional," she said, and he snorted a laugh. She arranged the peonies in a vase and turned to him with a smile. "Ready?"

He nodded.

"What?" she said.

"What what?"

"You're quiet."

"How would you know? We've never met before," he reminded her. She sighed. He grinned. "But it so happens I was deep in thought about something."

"Care to share with the class, Mr. Shepherd?"

"I was thinking you look incredible. New dress?"

She glanced down, cheeks flushing under his praise. In her quest to wear more color, she'd bought a form fitting little dress in royal blue. A bit of research revealed her skin did better in jewel tones instead of the earthy colors she'd always espoused. How she'd gone for twenty-six years without realizing that tidbit was anybody's guess. Shouldn't there be some kind of talk they gave to girls? Maybe in junior high they could discuss the birds and the bees and then do everybody's color panel. With the way her life had gone, the color panel would have been much more useful. And hair and makeup. Last night she'd stayed up obscenely late watching tutorials on YouTube that taught her more than she'd ever learned. Why was nobody imparting this wisdom? Twenty six years of naturally curly hair, and yet today marked the first time she had any realization what the diffuser on her hair dryer was for. For possibly the first time in her life she didn't look like she'd recently jabbed her finger in the light socket for kicks. And she'd managed a smoky eye with only two tries. The first try looked like she ran into a smoke-filled building to save small children and came out covered in melted charcoal, but that was what makeup remover was made for.

"This old thing? It probably looks new to you because we've never met before."

"That's undoubtedly why. Also, it still has the tag on it."

He pointed. She hiked up her arm, dropped her head to look, and spun in a circle like a dog trying to bite its own tail before realizing he'd been teasing her. She put her arm down. "I should tell you up front I don't like to be teased."

"I should tell you up front I only tease the people I like the most," he said, reaching out to give one of her curls a little tug. "Ready?"

Was she? She had no idea. "Yes?"

He took a step and paused. "Was that a question?"

"No?"

Rolling his eyes, he reached for her hand and tugged her behind him at a quick trot. He tucked her in the car and drove her to the town's lone diner, the same place she'd put on such a display for the town the previous night. She regarded him, eyes narrowed.

"The diner? My, what a convenient and centrally localized establishment."

"Would you shut it? I'll be a minute and I'll leave the air on so you don't suffocate." He parked the car, left it running, and got out. A minute later he returned with a bag of takeout containers.

"Picnic?" she guessed, somewhat hopefully. She had always wanted to go on a picnic.

"Wait and see," he said in a secretive little tone that sent shivers up and down her spine. "So, Miss Birdie, tell me about yourself."

"There's not a lot to tell, you know how it is. After a stint as an army ranger, I traveled around the world, trying to keep off the radar, until I stumbled into some trouble in a small town with an overbearing sheriff."

"That's the plot from *Rambo*," he said.

"I know, that's how I've been able to finance my fabulous lifestyle, by selling the rights to my story."

"You are such a loon. I swear, Birdie."

"What exactly do you swear, Duncan? Because you say it a lot, but there's never any follow up. You swear vengeance? Penitence? Retribution?"

He parked the car and faced her, leaning closer so he was only a whisper from her face. "I swear that someday I am going to take all the aggravation you've caused me every day of forever and give it back to you in spades. And then, Birdie Thompson, I'll have my retribution." His finger skimmed down her bare arm and she resisted the urge to shiver again.

"I'd be careful. I'm lethal."

"Baby, don't I know it." He reached into the back seat, picked up the bag of takeout, and got out of the car. She blinked, shaking her head to pull herself out of her haze, and followed him, noting their location for the first time.

"Grammy and Poppy's house?" Duncan's grandparents, Grammy and Poppy, were ubiquitous southern grandparents, adopted by the entire town who called them nothing other than Grammy and Poppy. Grammy was a throwback who believed in doing Halloween up right, with candy apples and popcorn balls. Every year Duncan, Sterling, and Birdie would go to their house before they started trick-or-treat. And without fail, Birdie ended up enjoying it even more than going door to door for candy. Along with Christmas and Easter, it was one of the only days she and Duncan buried the hatchet and enjoyed a peaceful day of celebration.

"Are they here?" she asked, half hopeful, half not. While she would love to visit, it might place undue expectations on them. One thing Birdie knew for certain—Grammy and Poppy would be thrilled by the match.

"No, they're with my aunt in Florida."

"Ah." He used his key to open the door, standing aside so she could enter. "Not to seem ungrateful, 'cause you know I love it here, but why are we here?"

"Because it's mine now."

She blinked at him. "You live with Grammy and Poppy?"

"No. I'm buying this house." He motioned around them.

It was a grand old farmhouse, two stories, massive rooms, a giant hearth. Whenever Birdie pictured her someday house, it was always this farm. "You're buying the farm? Why?"

"Grammy and Poppy have wanted to downsize for a long time, but it's hard to leave the old homestead, you know? I'm at the point in my life where I'm ready for a change, ready to settle down. It seemed like a natural fit." He pulled out a kitchen chair for her and set their bag of takeout on the table.

"I don't know what to say," she murmured.

"Mark it down, that's a first," he replied, but he was smiling.

"So this is what you do on dates," she said.

"No. I've never brought a girl to the farm before."

She huffed.

"What?" he said, tossing her a glance.

"Stop making me reevaluate things and see you as a human being," she said.

"No," he said.

They ate in companionable silence, a far cry from other meals they'd shared when he would steal her food or comment on what she shouldn't be eating. When their eyes happened to meet, he smiled and she felt her cheeks flush in response. What she'd said to him was true —he was a stupidly handsome man. Objectively he was better looking than Hayden, than even Sterling who had never lacked for female attention. And Birdie had never cared, had never seen him as anything more than a painful annoyance. But this Duncan—sweet, affectionate, thoughtful, a good kisser, was enough to sit up and take notice. And what she noticed was the way his long lashes swept over his cheeks every time he blinked, the way his thick, dark hair curled slightly at the temples, the quirk of his lush, full mouth.

"Look at you, looking at me," he said.

"You have barbecue sauce on your bottom lip," she said, a lie, but he grabbed for a napkin and dabbed furiously, unlike their former life when he would open his mouth and show her his masticated food for maximum annoyance.

"Did I get it?" he asked.

She shook her head. He dabbed harder while she reached over and filched the remainder of his cornbread. That was when he came to the realization she was lying and tossed his wadded napkin at her.

"Girl, you aggravate me." The way he said it, though, was anything but aggravated. They finished their meal. He stood and reached for her hand. "Come on a tour with me. I'm going to tell you my plans for the house."

"Tear it down and put up a parking lot?" she guessed. "Charge local businesses a fortune to use it?"

"Don't give me ideas," he said. They strolled through the house, hand in hand, while he told her what updates he planned, basically a modernization of the entire thing. It had fallen into minor disrepair of late, nothing earth shattering, but it would take a fair amount of time, care, and money to bring it back to par again.

"It sounds amazing," Birdie said dreamily "I can picture it exactly as it will be. You're on track to something good here, I think." She paused at the edge of the room, hands on hips as she surveyed the room.

"I think so, too," Duncan said. He edged closer and eased his arm around her neck, giving it a light squeeze. She faced him. It hadn't escaped her notice that the bedrooms upstairs were made up and ready for visitors. Was that what this was about? If so, he had another think coming. But even as she thought these things he kissed her cheek and took a step back. "Come on."

"Come where?" she asked.

"The next thing."

"What's the next thing?"

"The thing that happens after this one," he said.

She sighed, and he smiled, enjoying her annoyance. He kept her hand and led her to the car, tucking her inside. They drove to their former high school and parked. "Why are we here?"

"Shh, ya bother me," he said, leaving the car. She remained seated, confused, until he came for her, putting his hand in to help her out. He kept her hand again until they reached the door, then pulled out another key and unlocked it.

"Are you the mayor now? Where are you getting all these keys?" she whispered. Even though he had a key, it still felt like they were breaking in.

"Shh," he commanded.

"Tell me to shh one more time, Duncan, I dare you," she said, but it was lacking her usual rancor. Old Duncan seemed gone and the new one was all kinds of surprising. Birdie almost felt like she was following a stranger as he led her through a maze of halls and into the gymnasium, one that was partially lit with a little box on the floor.

"What is this?" she asked in a whisper.

"A re-do," he said.

"A re-do on what?" she asked. They reached the box. He pulled out his phone and set it inside, hitting a button so that soft music filtered out.

"A re-do on us, on something I regret."

Before she would have listed all the many things he had to regret, but this seemed too serious. "I can't imagine," she said instead.

He took a breath and picked up both her hands, clasping them in his. "Homecoming, my senior year. I saw you across the way, standing all alone, and I had the thought I should ask you to dance."

"You didn't," she said.

"I didn't."

"Because you were Mr. Popularity and I was uber geek," she affirmed, nodding sagely.

"No. Dancing with my best friend's geeky freshman sister probably would have earned me points with girls I was trying to impress with my sensitivity," he said, smiling.

"Then why not?" she said, because it seemed like he was waiting on her to ask.

"Because I somehow understood that if I ever danced with you, it would mean more than a throwaway homecoming favor. And I wasn't ready." He dropped her hands and took a tiny step forward, now holding one of his hands aloft. "Birdie Thompson, may I have this dance?"

She looked at his hand and back to his face, earnest and handsome and filled with something she had never seen before. "Yes," she said, placing her small palm in his larger one. He pulled her closer into a comfortable clasp and they started to dance, not talking, looking at each other, hearts thumping. It was so much more than Birdie ever expected of him. She had no idea what to do with all the new sensory input. Dancing. With Duncan. In their stinky high school gym. After a romantic speech. And a romantic dinner. At his beloved grandparents' family farm. Yowza.

CHAPTER 20

They danced a few songs and left the high school with a silent sort of urgency Birdie didn't understand. Her heart was thundering, hands shaking. Duncan tucked her inside the car, then jogged around to his side and slid behind the wheel. They sat in silence a few beats, both staring straight ahead, and then it was as if a dam broke between them. Maybe he reached for her, maybe she lunged for him. All Birdie knew was that she was once again in the parking lot of her high school, and this time she was the girl making out with a cute boy. And she didn't hate it, that was for certain.

They kissed like two people who had recently met up after a ten year absence marooned on opposing islands. Duncan pulled her into his lap and she obliged by yanking his shirt free of his pants and pressing her hands to his stomach. Birdie was not a shallow girl. Those abs, though.

His hands returned the favor by sliding under the hem of her skirt and resting on her knees, allowing his thumbs to caress her bare legs. Birdie shivered. "I should slap you for that," she said.

He laughed, lips moving against hers. "I could have you arrested for this," he said, indicating the way her hands were now gliding over his chest.

They kissed for a while longer, but Birdie began to sense him pulling away. He was still there, but the mood in the car shifted and she didn't know why. Usually she was the one overthinking things, but now it seemed to be Duncan's turn. At last he put his hands on her shoulders and physically eased her away.

"Birdie, we need to talk."

"You had twenty six years of talking. You should have said your piece then," she said, her lips chasing his. He kissed her a while longer and tried again.

"This is serious. I have to tell you something, something important."

His tone was newly ominous. She pulled back and studied his face, devoid of its usual rotten cockiness. "What?" she whispered, preemptive dread filling her chest. Whatever this was, it wouldn't be good.

He took a bracing breath. "Chelsea is pregnant."

She blinked at him. "Okay. Is that why Sterling's been freaking out? He could have told me."

He took another breath and swallowed convulsively. "The baby's not Sterling's."

"Chelsea cheated on Sterling? Wow. Okay. Whose baby is it?"

He blinked at her. She blinked back. "No," she said. He didn't contradict. She lunged for her purse, scrambling away from him. He tried to tug her back. She kicked him in the jaw. *Not hard enough,* she thought when he winced but otherwise didn't react. She flew out of the car and began walking. He didn't follow, but he did call to her.

"You can't walk home."

"I won't," she called in return.

"Sterling won't come. He won't pick up his phone," he said. "Get back in the car and I'll take you home, I swear."

She whirled on him. "Don't you ever talk to me again. Don't come near me, don't touch me, don't even look at me. I hate you." Her voice broke. She faced forward again and began marching, withdrawing her phone.

. . .

CAN YOU COME GET ME?

FIVE MINUTES LATER, Hayden arrived, pulled to the curb, and pushed open the door for her. She slid inside and faced forward. Neither of them said a word. He reached across the console and clasped her hand. She gripped it like a lifeline.

He took her to her house, opened the door, and ushered her inside. And then, as if he was the one who had been there a million times before, marched her down the hallway to her room, opened the door, and put her in her bed. And then he sat beside her, soothingly petting her head until, overcome by too many emotions to sort, she finally fell asleep.

In the morning, he was gone. A text on her phone was the only sign he'd been anything more than her imagination.

I CAN'T DO this anymore. I care about you, Birdie, you know I do. But I can't be part of another love triangle this soon, can't pick up the pieces of your heart when mine are still shattered. I wish you all the best.

BIRDIE TOOK A BREATH, squared her shoulders, and texted a reply. *I understand. Thank you for being there, for driving me home, for being a real friend. It's going to be a lucky girl who gets to be yours next, Hayden. Don't let it be too long. You're too good to sit on the shelf.* She added the robot emoji, hit send, and burst into tears.

She cried a long time and texted Sterling throughout. As Duncan predicted, he didn't text back, didn't pick up his phone when she called. For the first time ever, she called off work.

Shelley's voice was soothing and gentle. "Birdie, I know about Sterling and Duncan. You take as much time as you need, sweet girl."

"Thank you," Birdie replied, sniffling. The library was only open a few days a week, meaning it was her three day weekend anyway. She almost wished it weren't. Losing herself in the quiet softness of the library would feel soothing now. Unless maybe it wouldn't. Maybe she had now lost the ability to be soothed. She had lost both Duncan and Hayden. And her brother's heart was broken by the double betrayal. How could anything ever be right again?

Duncan called and texted. She rejected his attempts, finally blocking him and deleting his number. Not surprisingly, he eventually showed up in her room.

"Go away," she said, tossing a book at him and missing completely.

"No."

"I hate you."

"So you said, but there's a problem," he said.

"What could be a bigger problem than you getting my brother's girlfriend pregnant?" she asked.

"It's Sterling. He's gone."

She sat up. "What do you mean gone?"

"I mean gone, Birdie. Checked out. Disappeared without a trace."

"He wouldn't do that."

"He did."

She glanced at her phone, remembering all the calls and texts she'd aimed toward her brother. She tried another one. *Where are you?* There was no answer. "When is the last time someone saw him?"

Duncan lifted one shoulder. "Couple of days ago."

"Does he know?"

Duncan nodded. "Chelsea told him."

"How long have you known?"

He swallowed hard and wouldn't make eye contact. "Couple of months."

Her gut knifed with pain. He knew. Long before he pursued her, he knew what he'd done to Sterling. It wasn't about her right now, it was about Sterling. Her feet swung off the bed. "I'm going to find him."

"How?"

"I don't know."

"I'm helping," he declared.

"No, you've done enough and he won't want to see you. You're why he went away."

He flinched but didn't back down. "I know, but I'm still going."

She scowled at him as she texted Hayden.

I'M SO sorry to bug you, but I have a quick question. When is the last time you saw Sterling leaving his shop?

THREE DAYS AGO. Why?

HE'S MISSING.

AH. Probably holed up somewhere. Do you have access to his credit card receipts?

YES, I'll try that. Thank you.

LMK if you need anything else.

SHE SIGHED, wishing she could need him for everything. She couldn't, though. It wasn't fair. She had forfeited the privilege of her friendship with him. Because of Duncan, another thing he had taken from her. *I'm sure we'll get it figured out, but thanks. Take care.*

YOU, too.

. . .

So polite, so impersonal. It hurt like Hayden had once described, like an amputation. She reached for her laptop and began to type. Duncan perched on the edge of her bed. She wanted to kick him off but was too immersed in typing. The beauty of doing her brother's accounting work was that she had ready access to all his records. She brought up his favored credit card and scanned.

"He got a hotel room in Daytona yesterday. He ate at a café there today." She stood and closed her laptop, reaching for her suitcase instead.

"What are you doing?" Duncan asked.

"What does it look like I'm doing? I'm going after him."

He stood. "I'm going with you."

"Nope."

"Yes. He's my best friend."

Her head jerked up, eyes snapping fire. "What kind of best friend sleeps with his girlfriend?"

"The stupid kind. But I'm still going. He's my responsibility as much as he is yours."

"Fine. Whatever. I'll be packed and ready in an hour."

"I'm packed and ready now, my bag's in the car. And we're taking my car."

"No," she said.

"Stop arguing just because you're mad at me. Your decrepit clunker won't make it out of Georgia."

His car was nice and new, the weasel. "Wait for me outside. I can't look at you," she said, voice breaking.

"Birdie," he said softly. His hand reached out. She remained focused on her task, tossing things haphazardly into her case. He dropped his hand and walked away, closing the door as he left. Birdie dumped the suitcase and began putting things in with thought and care, things she'd actually need.

Less than an hour later, she was packed. She left her mother a note, something vague about a last-minute getaway with Duncan and Sterling. There was no way she could tell her mother the truth. It was their way to pussyfoot around their father's moods and protect their mother from any harshness or too much reality. Goodness knew she'd had too much of it already, more than enough for a lifetime.

Duncan took her bag, popped the trunk, and dropped it inside. He slid behind the wheel and faced her. "Ready?"

She gave a curt nod, not looking at him. He cranked the car, but before he could reverse, the back door opened and closed. They turned to look and saw Hayden sitting sedately on the seat.

"What are you doing?" Duncan exclaimed. "Get out of my car."

"No," Hayden said, tone and expression resolute.

Birdie swallowed hard, heart aflutter.

"Seriously, what are you doing here, Paxton? Are you nuts?" Duncan said.

"I'm going with you," Hayden said.

"Why on earth would you do that?" Duncan asked.

Hayden's eyes landed on Birdie. "Because he's my best friend," she whispered and he smiled a little. Duncan looked between them.

"What on earth? Birdie, have you ever so much as talked to him in your life?" Duncan demanded. Her mouth quirked, echoed by Hayden's amused smile.

"Not a word," she admitted. "Nonetheless I need him."

"And I'm staying," Hayden added.

Duncan faced forward, flummoxed. "I don't think…" he began.

"No, you don't, do you, Duncan?" Birdie interrupted, lips pressed together in a grim line. He took note of her expression, the pain and sadness in her eyes, and put his hand on the gearshift.

"Let me go on the record and say I don't foresee this ending well. And it's weird."

"I think we can all agree on that," Birdie murmured.

In the back seat, Hayden laughed.

CHAPTER 21

It occurred to Birdie, as they started to drive, that Hayden might not know what happened. With something akin to panic, she pulled out her phone and sent him a text.

You should probably not be here.

You want me to go? he returned.

No, of course I want you. But this is going to hit too close to home. Duncan got Sterling's girlfriend pregnant. Swallowing a lump, she sent the painful text.

The text bubbles disappeared three times before Hayden finally replied.

. . .

I KNOW.

BIRDIE'S HEAD SNAPPED UP, staring straight ahead. He knew. He knew how similar the painful situation was to his own and came anyway. For her.

"What are you doing?" Duncan asked as Birdie began scrambling over the seat divider into the back.

"Tradin' up," she replied. She sat and circled Hayden in a crushing hug, resting her head on his shoulder. He leaned over her and buckled her into her seatbelt before kissing the top of her head and resting his against it.

"What on earth is going on?" Duncan murmured, and this time Hayden and Birdie both smiled.

* * *

THEY DROVE for three hours in stony silence that should have been tense but wasn't with Hayden there. Birdie was used to being silent with him and found it soothing, even now in the middle of her biggest crisis to date.

So. What happened on the date? Must have been epic.

BIRDIE STARED at her phone with a sigh. She didn't want to tell him. He nudged her.

HONESTY FOREVER, remember?

WITH ANOTHER SIGH, she replied. *It went well, at least at first. A romantic stroll down memory lane. He seemed to be making great strides to be a grownup, something that had been lacking all these years. And then...well, you know. You can imagine how that bombshell announcement went over.*

Don't have to imagine. *I lived it.*

I'm so sorry, *sorry to be the cause of dredging all of it up again.*

Stop apologizing *for things beyond your control. Or else.*

She eyed him. *Or else what? You'll withdraw again?*

Can't, *apparently. I'm in this friendship thing too deep.*

She gave his leg a pat. From the front, Duncan sighed.

Our chauffer doesn't *like it when you touch me.*

Ask me if I care, she replied.

I care, *but in a good way.* He gave her leg a little pat. Duncan sighed again.

How did *you know we were going away?* she asked.

. . .

BECAUSE WHEN I was in Sterling's shoes, I ran away, too. And you're you; of course you'd go after him.

I WOULD HAVE FOR YOU, too, if I'd known you then. My circle is small, but it's for life. I don't let anyone go. Her glance landed on the back of Duncan's head. How could she possibly continue to be friends with him after this? On the other hand, how could she not?

Likely guessing her thoughts, Hayden reached out and clasped her hand, giving it a reassuring squeeze. She rested her head on his shoulder again, sighing. She was peripheral to the current drama, and yet it hurt her soul on a molecular level. The only thing getting her through at the moment was him. How must he have felt, being one of the central players and all alone?

HOW DID you get through it? she texted.

I WAS NOT in good shape when I came home. And then help arrived in the most unexpected package—the little sister of my sworn enemy.

OOH, sworn enemy. That sounds very dramatic.

I KNOW how much you enjoy the high drama, he typed, and she chortled. Duncan sighed and she chortled harder.

I CAN'T POSSIBLY GET ENOUGH. It's what I live for.

HOLD ON TO THAT SENTIMENT. 'Cause when we reach Daytona, it's about to hit the fan.

. . .

I'll take it, as long as it means I get Sterling back safe and well.

135

HE EASED his arm around her shoulders and gave them a squeeze. Duncan whipped onto the exit and barked, "We're stopping for lunch, if you two can peel yourselves apart for a minute."

"I suppose," Hayden said in a lazy tone. "But only for a minute."

CHAPTER 22

"I don't understand this," Duncan said, facing Hayden and Birdie on opposing sides of the fast food table.

"There's nothing to understand. We're friends," Birdie replied tiredly, staring doggedly at her food. It hurt too much to look at Duncan now, knowing what he'd done to Sterling, what he'd done to her.

"Birdie, can't you look at me?" Duncan asked with uncharacteristic softness.

She shook her head. He drew in a sharp breath.

"We weren't even together then," he tried. "It's not like I cheated on *you*."

"I cannot, will not do this right now. Finding Sterling is our first priority, our only priority."

"Fine, then at least explain this to me. You two haven't spoken a solitary word to each other in three hours, yet you're all over each other."

Birdie's head snapped up, cheeks flaming. "We are not all over each other."

Duncan flicked a hand at them, indicating Hayden's hand where it rested comfortingly on her knee.

"It's called affection," she said. "I am a deeply affectionate person."

"Since when?"

"Since always."

"Never with me."

"You don't make it easy to be soft around you because you're always so hard on me, but there have been plenty of times," she pointed out.

"Name one."

"Sophomore year basketball tryouts. Sterling got on and you got cut." His lashes fluttered, remembering that when Sterling left the room, she'd tackled him in a hug. "Junior year Anna Mosby broke up with you because her parents said she couldn't date a white boy. You tried to blow it off, but I knew you were secretly sad so I insisted we watch *Backdraft* so you'd have a legitimate reason to cry. Do you want me to go on?"

His eyes flicked to Hayden, embarrassed. "No. I still don't understand. You never said a word about this."

"Apparently there's a lot we don't tell each other," she said. She could hear the bitterness in her tone and didn't like it. She stuffed a fry in her mouth to make it stop talking. Eventually, she would get over this. At the moment, the pain was too raw.

They finished their meal in awkward silence and walked back to the car. Duncan held the passenger door for Birdie. She bypassed him and climbed in the back with Hayden. Duncan sighed and they were back on their way.

Two hours later, they arrived in Daytona Beach.

Duncan had already used his powers of persuasion, AKA sweet talking, to get the clerk to tell them Sterling's room number. They bypassed the desk and took the elevator to the seventh floor. Birdie led the way. Hayden was naturally subdued, there only as backup support for her. Duncan was both guilty and nervous and trying not to be. Birdie knew exactly how it would be when Sterling opened the door. She would have to step up and play referee and peacemaker, and the thought made her preemptively weary.

She knocked and knocked again, harder. Hayden reached out and knocked with authority. Birdie studied his profile. Was man knocking a thing? Would the extra power and authority actually work to summon her brother? Apparently because he pulled open the door and did the squinting blink of someone who had just been yanked from sleep.

"Birdie, what are you doing here?" he garbled.

"Appreciating being the better looking sibling for the first time in our lives," she said, taking stock of his rough appearance—unshaved, unkempt, sallow.

He shook his head as if trying to throw off water droplets. The smells from the room began to eek out—sweat, BO, alcohol, and vomit. Was he drunk or merely hung-over? She guessed they bled into each other so seamlessly he didn't even know the answer. Slothlike, his attention swiveled to Hayden beside her.

"What's he doing here?"

"Who? I came alone."

Sterling blinked at her, confused and possibly a touch panicked. Hayden laughed, causing Duncan to shift and sigh and that was when Sterling's eyes lighted on him.

"Get out."

"No," Duncan replied. Apparently instead of being meek, he was going to play it as stubborn hardhead.

Sterling barreled forward, knocking Birdie into the doorframe. Hayden put out a restraining arm, barring Sterling from leaving the room.

"Let's take this outside," he suggested.

"No," Sterling said. He shook him off but took a step back. "I'm not leaving this room. He can go. I have nothing to say to him."

"Yes, you do," Hayden argued. "And we're taking it outside."

"I'm not," Sterling stubbornly insisted. Birdie wondered if it had been a mistake to bring Hayden because he was making Sterling react like a stubborn teenager.

"You are. Want to know why?" Hayden put his arm around Birdie's shoulders and pulled her against him. "Because your sweet little sister here is under the mistaken impression you're not a complete waste of space, and I don't think you want to disillusion her right now. Do you, Saint Sterling?"

Sterling scowled, blinking hard at Birdie. His shoulders sagged. Hayden turned his attention on Duncan. "Move it."

"You can't..." Duncan began, but Hayden preempted him.

"I don't think you want to know what I can and can't, Shepherd. If you want this to work, you need to for once in your life shut up and take direction. Get moving."

Miraculously, Duncan pressed his lips together and turned toward the elevator. Hayden followed, Birdie snagged Sterling's arm and brought up the rear. They piled into the elevator together and faced forward. Somehow Birdie was now in the lead, the three of them behind her, tense and menacing.

"So this is how it feels to lead a gang," Birdie mused.

Hayden snickered, reached out, and gently squeezed the back of her neck. Now Sterling and Duncan both sighed and Birdie tossed Hayden a smile. He gave her a little wink and she linked her arm with his.

They left the hotel by the back, stumbling out onto the beach like moles getting their first taste of sunlight. Even though it was routinely sunny and a hundred degrees where they lived, there was something especially intense about the way the sun sparkled off the ocean. Squinting, they made their way toward the roaring surf. It was low tide, with long stretches of pressed sand, easier to walk on than the fluffy portions of sand. Birdie held Hayden's arm while she plucked off her shoes. Her pause seemed to spark Sterling and Duncan who faced each other and pounced, now tussling in the sand like warring crabs.

Birdie yelped and covered her mouth, clutching Hayden's arm. He gave it a reassuring pat, telling her this was somehow acceptable. It wasn't as if she hadn't ever seen them tussle. During adolescence, pouncing on each other and wrestling seemed to be their preferred mode of showing affection. They tried tackling Birdie only one time. She burst into tears and they both got into trouble. But this was something altogether different. Then it had seemed gentle, teasing. Now they were both out for blood, grunting when their punches landed. Sterling's lip was split and Duncan's eye puffed. Eventually it was like watching Hayden's robot wind down. The hits started missing their targets, whiffing into air, the back and forth wrestling grew slower until finally they both lay on their backs, sweating, covered in sand and blood.

"We are done," Sterling panted.

"No," Duncan said. He tried to sound belligerent but only sounded pained. Sterling tried to lunge for him again, but Hayden intervened, picking both of them up by their scruffs like errant puppies.

"I think y'all have had enough of beating on each other for the moment. Nobody is winning at this point. Don't think I didn't enjoy it, though." He released them a few feet apart and kept his stance between them, offering neutrality but holding them back, nonetheless.

"How?" Sterling asked, pain now replacing all the anger.

Duncan huffed out a breath and ran his hand through his hair. "Not on purpose, okay? I would never purpose to do that."

"Then how?" Sterling repeated.

"It was at that party a few months ago in Terrytown. You couldn't go. Your dad. I was drunk. I saw Chelsea and asked her to dance." He held up his hand in supplication. "Not because I was hitting on her. She was a familiar face and she looked out of place. We started to dance and she said…" he broke off and looked away.

"Said what?" Sterling pressed, still pulsing with anger.

Duncan swallowed convulsively and darted Birdie a glance before returning his eyes to Sterling. "She asked me if I was ever going to tell Birdie I was in love with her. I didn't like it, made me mad. I kissed her as a punishment, to shut her up. But she was drunk, too. She kissed me back and…things just happened. I'm sorry. You have to know I'm sorry. I would never do that if I had been thinkin', if I had been in my right mind. We both regret it, don't even like each other, you know that." Eyes watery now, he sniffled and looked away, toward the ocean.

Sterling regarded him in silence a minute before answering. "I don't know if I can ever get over this."

Wisely for once, Duncan didn't reply. His lips trembled, and he pressed them together, crossing his arms over his chest, holding himself tightly together. They stood together in silence a moment, the roar of the ocean the only sound. Birdie knew Sterling would forgive eventually, if only because he had no one else. Duncan was his person, had always been his person. One couldn't function without the other. The realization made her feel both heartened and alone. She was glad for them, but it was also a painful reminder she had always been the outsider in their trio. Hayden's thumb smoothed on her forearm where his hand still rested and her face tipped studying him. He regarded her with silent concern. *Are you okay?* She nodded and smiled and then beamed, tossing her arms around him and hugging fiercely. *He* was her person. Maybe they didn't have three decades together like Duncan and Sterling, but they had mutual understanding, affection, and support. All the things that made friendship good, that made life good.

Hayden returned her tight hug, kissing the top of her head.

"What is this about?" Sterling asked, puzzled as he gawked at them.

"Apparently they're a thing," Duncan said.

"Puh, what? No," Sterling said. For the moment they were once again united in their mutual hatred of Hayden.

"We are not a thing; we are friends," Birdie protested.

"Yeah, I routinely hug and kiss my friends like that," Duncan said, full sarcasm.

"Maybe you should," Birdie suggested, pointing between him and Sterling. The two men regarded each other with a scowl.

"I'm not there yet," Sterling said.

"I'll never be there," Duncan returned, and Sterling gave another little puff of laughter.

"You two are a mess. In all the ways. *All the ways*. Why don't you go get cleaned up?" Birdie suggested. "It's called soap and a shower, big brother. Try it. You'll thank me later."

Sterling eased forward, plucked her from Hayden's grasp, twirled her around, and covered her face with kisses. "You don't like my stink, Birdie?"

"Gross, boy germs, cooties," Birdie squealed, squirming, but she was giggling as ever when Sterling was affectionate. She squeezed him and kissed his cheek in return before he set her down. Tentatively, he and Duncan took a step toward the building. "Can I trust you two not to brawl until we get back in there?"

"We'll see how it goes," Duncan returned, but he sounded upbeat.

Hayden and Birdie watched them go in silence and regarded each other. She glanced at the long sprawl of beach beside them. Hayden shucked out of his shoes and picked them up, clasping Birdie's hand with his free one. They turned and started to walk.

CHAPTER 23

They walked for a long, long time in total silence. Birdie's mind felt peaceful for the first time in what felt like forever. She had no idea why she and Hayden refused to talk to each other. If anyone asked her to articulate a reason, she wouldn't be able to come up with one. All she could say for certain was that she liked it. And when the silence finally broke, she felt like it would be momentous. Right now, in the middle of a family crisis, was not their moment.

Their arms swung companionably between them, hands clasped. Hayden stopped suddenly, dropped her fingers, and bent, scraping something in the sand. He picked up a little mound and held it out to her. Birdie peered closer and gasped at the live sand dollar in his palm. She held up her hands, palms cupped. He dropped it carefully into her grasp and brushed his hands. She tipped her head studying it. She had only ever seen them in stores, dried out and bleached. Alive and unharmed was so much better.

When she looked up, Hayden was watching her instead of the sand dollar, eyes kindling and intense. She froze and swallowed hard, licking her lips. His eyes traced the movement, pulse leaping. She so badly wanted to set aside the little creature, wrap her arms around him, and kiss him until the pain went away. But that would be unfair. So she smiled and stooped to resettle the creature in the sand. When she stood, she clasped his hand and turned them back around, toward the hotel. Hayden gave her hand a squeeze, as if he understood and agreed. *That was close, but we're not ready.* She squeezed his hand in return. *Someday, maybe.*

They reached the hotel room but before Birdie could knock, the door was yanked open.

"Need to talk to you," Duncan declared, snagging her hand and giving her a tug farther into the hallway. Hayden frowned, regarding her with a questioning flick of his eyebrow. She gave him a little nod and he went inside.

Duncan ran his fingers through his wet hair, upending it. "You're a hypocrite, you know it, Birdie?"

"How, pray tell," she said, crossing her arms over her chest.

"You're so mad at me for this thing with Chelsea, and all the while you've been cheating on me. With *Paxton.*" He snarled as if he'd mentioned a flaming dung heap.

She uncrossed her arms and pressed her fingers to her temples. "Where to begin? First of all, you and I were never together. I told you repeatedly there were other considerations and I needed time."

"So that night in my car, when you were all over me, practically tearing my clothes off, that was us not being together?" he countered.

Her fingers migrated to her cheeks, trying to press the hot blood out of them. "For the love, lower your voice." She was humiliated over the memory of those kisses, over how close she had come to losing control with *Duncan,* a person who could apparently cut her so deeply and not even realize or care.

"I will not," he yelled.

"You will," she hissed, hand settling on his chest and giving it a hard shove. "How dare you try to accuse me, to drag me down to your level? You are the heartless, faithless one in this scenario, not me. Hayden and I are not together, as I've repeatedly told you. We are friends, unlike us."

He blanched. "What are you talking about? Of course we're friends. We've always been friends."

"We have never been friends," she said, and now her voice was rising. "You have teased me and picked at me and bullied me my entire life. You gave me a nickname I loathe, you criticized what I ate, the way I dressed, my lack of physical fitness. You made fun of me for reading, for thinking, for *being.* You think I'm still a kid because I live with my mom. Well, guess what? I'm not the one still getting drunk every weekend like a frat boy on hiatus."

"Birdie," he breathed, swallowing hard. "How could you have everything so wrong?"

"Explain to me how I'm wrong," she demanded.

"You are, have always been, one of my favorite people, one of my best friends. Teasing you was my way of showing you how much I care. You know who else I nicknamed? No one, only you. You make me laugh, you make me crazy, you make me think, you challenge me in all the ways. I got so angry when Chelsea asked me that question because..." he paused and swallowed again. "Because it's true. I love you, Birdie."

They regarded each other in heavy silence. Hayden opened the door and poked his head out, checking on her. She held up a finger and he stepped back, holding the door for her.

"You have a funny way of showing it," she said softly to Duncan before turning to follow Hayden inside.

For supper they ordered pizza and ate in the room while watching TV. Sports, naturally. With three men, Birdie could hardly expect anything different. She and Hayden sat shoulder to shoulder on one bed. Duncan and Sterling sat on the other, far apart, shoulders hunched in shared misery and tension.

How are you holding up?

She glanced at Hayden, still apparently engrossed in the game. If she hadn't received the text from him, she might not believe he even noticed his phone.

You are one subliminal texter. How are you doing this?

Magic, he texted back, wagging his brows.

I'm beginning to believe you are.

It's my one great talent, to text with no one noticing. I'm a one trick pony. So fun at parties!

You'd be the person I gravitate to at parties, for certain. To answer your question, I'm fine. My concern here is Sterling. How are you? I can't help but believe this is rehashing a lot of pain for you.

It is, but it's also somehow strangely cathartic, if that makes sense. Seeing them brawl makes me realize I never got that sort of closure with my friend. Going to track him down, punch his lights out.

I'd think you were joking, but boys are crazy.

We are, but usually because of some woman.

She laughed, causing Duncan and Sterling to dart her puzzled frowns. *Now I can't wish you no future craziness because I'd be dooming you to eternal aloneness.*

It's a catch-22 for certain. Sweet peace or a sweet-smelling girl? Seems we men can't have both in this life.

I'd accuse you of being cynical, but you have precedent. Serious question: do you really think it's worth it? Look at you, at Sterling, eaten up with pain. Why do we willingly do this to ourselves? Isn't it better to be alone than to hurt this way?

He pondered a bit before he replied. *I felt that way soon after, swore off women forever. But...* He turned to survey her, his eyes sweeping up and down before lingering affectionately on her face. She put up a hand and pressed it to his cheek. He turned his face, kissing her palm.

Someone from the other bed cleared his throat pointedly. Birdie dropped her hand and faced forward, reaching for her phone.

Seems like a strange compulsion, running headlong toward disaster on the off chance it might work, might not end in pain.

Maybe because the moments between are just that good, he suggested.

That's what my mom said.

Moms are usually right about these things, he replied.

You smell as good as you look and feel, in case I've never said. I should probably have it engraved or tattooed somewhere.

Birdie, same. He took a deep breath, held it, and let it out slowly. It might have been a frustrated sound except she knew he was surreptitiously sniffing her.

We could be those friends who are always there for each other, who never make it anything more. Like Jessica Fletcher and Seth Hazlitt.

I'm sorry, are you referencing Murder She Wrote *to encapsulate our amazing relationship?*

Would you prefer Columbo? *Because I don't know who his best friend was, and I doubt she was a girl.*

Girl, you have quirkiness all sewn up. And if you think Jessica and Seth were only friends, you are out of your ever-loving mind.

What? No way. She dated all those other men. The elderly Irish secret agent, Lumiere from Beauty and The Beast. *I know Seth, okay? No way he would have stood by while she was with all those other men.*

Maybe he was a very patient man. Maybe he was waiting for the right moment. Or maybe he knew Jessica was worth waiting for. Probably all of those things.

Good man, Seth Hazlitt. Maybe the best man. She linked her arm with his and rested her head on his shoulder. He patted her leg, tilting his head to rest on hers.

Duncan jumped off the bed and turned off the TV. "How are we divvying up sleeping arrangements?"

"Well, as I'm the one paying for the room, this is my bed," Sterling said, giving it a pat. "And Birdie gets the other 'cause she's a girl and the only one I like here."

"I think I should share the bed with Birdie," Duncan declared. Everyone stared at him, blinking. "Clearly Sterling doesn't want me in his bed."

"What makes you think I want you in mine?" Birdie asked.

"Don't you?" he asked with all of his former cocky smugness. A month ago she would have laughed at him. But now, with a new understanding of how her body responded to him, of the way it felt to touch him, to kiss him and be kissed in return, she remained mute, scowling. His look began to morph into a triumphant smile. She reached for her shoe, intending to pelt it at him.

"What's the point of trying?" he goaded. "Your aim is off by a mile."

Hayden tugged off her shoe and pelted it at him, hitting him hard in the chest. He and Birdie high fived.

"Hey," Duncan said.

The tension dialed down when Sterling burst forth in a surprised guffaw of laughter.

CHAPTER 24

In the end, Sterling grudgingly allowed Duncan to share his bed. It wasn't as if it hadn't happened before, at countless and untold sleepovers, practically since their birth. Birdie took the other bed, and Hayden arranged a little pallet on the floor.

Duncan and Sterling were both fast and heavy sleepers, the kind who could light no matter where or no matter when. Birdie waited for their heavy breathing and then peeped over the side of her bed. Hayden stared up at her, grinning. She lifted her covers, scooting aside when he eased in beside her, and then she was stuck. *Now what?* She had never shared the bed with a man before, unless one counted Sterling when they were little and used to share a space when they visited their grandparents.

Hayden seemed to be having similar regrets. He stared up at the ceiling, body tense. Birdie's hand migrated the short distance between them, seeking his. Their fingers touched. He latched on, then rolled to face her. She did the same, their clasped hands now resting between them. It was an intimate thing to lie with a man face to face, to offer oneself up in the most vulnerable position. His free hand reached out and caressed her earlobe. Birdie arched instinctively toward him, like a cat. His arm stretched across her waist and dragged her beside him, aligning her back against him, big spoon to little spoon. Birdie nestled, settling in, enjoying the possessive weight of his arm on her waist. This, then, was what her mother had been talking about, this intimate sense of belonging with another person. *I could get used to this,* she thought. Followed by, *Sterling and Duncan are going to kill me when they wake up and see.* And then, *Ask me if I care.*

An unknown time later, her eyes popped open. Hayden's arm was still tucked cozily over her middle. She raised her head, looking for the clock. They'd been asleep two hours. She was about to lie back down when she realized half the bed across from her was empty, covers tossed aside. Gently, she eased out from under Hayden's arm and perched on the edge of her bed, straining closer to see. In the darkness, Sterling and Duncan looked alike—same dark hair and muscled bodies. On closer inspection, Duncan was the one still sleeping.

Birdie eased from the bed and started for the bathroom when she felt a slight breeze. Turning, she saw the door to the balcony slightly ajar. Thinking Sterling might have stepped out for some air, she tiptoed there and soundlessly opened the door. What she saw made her heart drop to her toes. Her brother sat perched on the balcony looking for all the world like he was about to let go and jump.

"Sterling." She whispered it softly, so as not to startle him, even though what she wanted to do was scream his name as she dashed forward and peeled him off the edge.

"Go back inside," he said, voice strained.

"No. Come down, come with me."

He shook his head. The motion tipped his balance. He caught the edge to avoid falling off.

"Sterling, you're starting to frighten me. Please get down."

"I'm so tired," he said instead. "So tired."

She glanced back inside the room. No way to raise the alert without alarming Sterling. Instead she stepped out, hefted herself onto the high rail, and perched beside him.

"What are you doing?" he snapped. "Get down off here."

"You go, I go," she said. She tried to sound brave, but her voice shook, as did everything else. They were seven stories off the ground, well high enough to die if they fell. Birdie wasn't the type to enjoy heights. Or risks. She hated roller coasters. Perching on the edge of a rail seventy feet above the ground was the greatest sort of risk. But tapping into Sterling's big brother instinct was the only way she could think of to distract him. "Now, why are you tired? What are you tired from?"

"Everything," he said, voice husky. "I'm tired of doing all the things, of being all the things. Duncan gets to screw up, gets to live however he wants, and Chelsea still chose him."

"Really, Sterling? You're making Duncan your yardstick?" Birdie said, tone dry.

He gave a little grunt of amusement.

"And Chelsea didn't choose him. She drunkenly stumbled into him, which is another reason I can't stand her. She has remarkably bad taste. Clearly you are the better choice in that scenario."

"It's not just Chelsea. I mean it is, that hurts, but it's everything." He drew a shaky breath. "I don't want to turn into Dad, Birdie."

"You won't."

"You can't know that. Haven't you ever watched those old videos of Dad and thought how much he looks like me, sounds like me, *acts like me*? He didn't start out crazy or Mom wouldn't have married him. When did it happen? When did he lose his mind?"

"Sterling, that won't be you, I swear it," Birdie said fervently.

"Look at me, Birdie. I'm falling apart. I ran away from home and now I'm..." He shook his head.

"Hey," she said gently. "You might be depressed. You might even be manic-depressive. But you will never be Dad. Want to know how I know?"

"How?" he asked, voice a tiny little quiver, so much like when he was a little boy and had hurt feelings.

"Because you have never once made me feel the way Dad has made me feel our whole lives. Dad is mentally ill, yes, and that's hard, it's hard on all of us. Probably you the most because you take the brunt. But Dad is also selfish. He refuses to get care, to go to the doctor, to try medication or counseling. He *likes* to wallow, enjoys the little power plays, wants Mom to stay alone and pining him forever for the sake of his ego. You are not like Dad, Sterling. If anyone is like Dad, it's..." she trailed off as a realization hit her, so startling and sudden that she flinched and had to grip the rail to avoid toppling off.

"Birdie," Sterling said, and now he flinched and had to grip and they were both startlingly, precariously close to falling. At least until strong arms circled them from behind, pulling them both back onto the balcony.

"What are you doing? What are you thinking?" Duncan demanded. He was the one holding Sterling. He let him go, giving Sterling a little shove. "Don't ever do that again."

Hayden had hold of Birdie, soothing her with his touch, one arm gripping her tightly while the other ran up and down her spine. She shuddered, pressing her cheek to his heart.

"I needed a moment to think, is all," Sterling said, a lie absolutely no one bought.

"Well, don't," Duncan said. "If you're mad at me, be mad. Hit me again, but don't..." His words cut off, voice breaking. "Don't. Please?"

Sterling clamped his jaw tight and looked away, toward the ocean. "I need to talk to Birdie some more."

No one moved. "Yes," Birdie said, knowing Hayden was waiting on her say so to let her go.

"Can we trust you not to do anything else stupid?" Duncan asked.

Sterling gave him a curt nod.

"What about you, Chi...Birdie?" Duncan asked.

"I only went up there to talk to him," she said, annoyed that he might think she was considering ending it all because of him. As if. She wrinkled her nose in disgust. His cheek twitched and he winked at her. She shoved him and he laughed as he stepped inside.

"What's up with you two?" Sterling asked. He sank to a sitting position, resting his back against the door.

"Which one?" she asked, following suit and aligning her body with his so they were shoulder to shoulder.

"Either, both."

She blew out a breath. "Hayden and I have been texting for a while. We're friends."

He took that in stride, nodding.

"And Duncan has been showing up, pursuing me. I kissed him. A lot. We had a date. It was epic, and then epically bad." She rested her chin on her knees. Sterling did the same.

"There was a time when I would have been thrilled by that information. I used to have a secret dream you two would end up together. I long suspected he had a thing for you, but it was on the list of things we never talked about."

"And now?" she asked.

"Believe it or not, I think Paxton might be the better choice."

"Me too, but it doesn't matter. He's got a lot going on. Apparently being cheated on by your significant other with your best friend is all the rage with handsome young men these days."

"I'd ask him for pointers on how to get through it, if he didn't hate me so much."

"Do you know why he hates you?"

"Lots of reasons, probably," he mused.

"One specifically. It's because you put on the perfect guy façade. He thinks it's fake."

"It is," Sterling admitted, as if imparting a painful secret.

"I know. But guess what? I love you the most anyway, still worship you like a hero. You have done more for me than anybody in my life, and for that I am very sorry." She swallowed hard.

He turned to look at her. "Sorry? Birdie, what on earth are you talking about?"

"You take care of all of us, Sterling, and it's too much. I never meant to be a liability. I've been trying hard to pull my own weight lately."

"Is that where you've been? Is that why you're ignoring me, not showing up?"

She nodded.

He laughed and pressed his hand over his eyes. "Man, Birdie, when you're wrong, you're really wrong. I have never, in our entire lives, considered you a liability. You're my partner in crime, the only other person who understands what it's like to be a kid in our family. You have always lightened the load, always made me laugh, pulled my head up when I started to get bogged down. You help with Mom and Dad in innumerable ways, and I have been so, so lonely without you these last few weeks." He sniffled.

Birdie did him one better by bursting into tears and pelting herself at his chest. He wrapped her in a tight hug and cried in return, wetting her hair with his tears.

"I'm sorry," she murmured.

"Me, too," he agreed.

"What are you sorry for?"

"For all of it. For trying to be perfect, for not letting you in and telling you when I'm sinking, when I need help. For the way our family is and the toll it's taken on you. The way Dad is with you, Birdie. I swear sometimes I want to kill him."

"Sterling, hey, it's okay. You know why?" She peeled back and looked in his face. "Because I have you. I have always had you, to run interference, to bolster me, to be my champion. As long as I have you and Mom on my side, I can do anything, even overcome the complete disinterest of the man who's supposed to love me most. And you haven't exactly had it easy being in the center of his adoration. He put too many expectations on you, pressured you to be who he wanted you to be so he could live vicariously."

Sterling nodded his agreement. She smiled, pressed her palms to his cheeks, and kissed his forehead. "Now, sweetest big brother, what are we going to do about your stupid pregnant ex and your stupid best friend?"

Sterling gave a watery little laugh and slung his arm over her shoulder. "I don't know. Right now I hate them both."

"Me, too. Thompson hating power, ignite." She stuck up her hand and he high fived it.

"I don't want to stay that way, though. It's not heal…"

She pressed her palm to his mouth. "Of course it's not, and of course you won't. You'll get over it and be magnanimous because that's who you are and that's why we love you. But just for a little while, let's focus on all the ways we hate them. And all the ways we could take our revenge. I'm thinking of a plot that involves dousing them with honey and leaving them for the fire ants."

Sterling laughed hard. "I have somethin' worse."

She sat up, expectant smile on her face. "What?"

He leaned closer to whisper. "We could let them have each other."

Birdie giggled. "That's diabolical. I love it."

They sat on the balcony for hours, until the sun came up, talking, laughing, plotting painful endings for both Chelsea and Duncan. It was cleansing, but even so Birdie knew there was something painful she needed to say.

She clasped his hand and gave it a squeeze, not sure if she was trying to give strength or siphon it. "Sterling, you really scared me tonight."

"I'm sorry," he said in a choked, embarrassed whisper.

"I don't need an apology, and I don't want promises not to do it in the future. What I want is an honest answer. If I hadn't found you, would you have...?"

He nodded, sniffling as tears ran down his face.

"Do you need help?"

He nodded again, crying harder.

She hugged him, pressing her face to his. "Then let's find some," she whispered.

CHAPTER 25

In the end, Sterling agreed to a voluntary psychiatric hold at the hospital in the next town over from their home. Hayden drove his car while Birdie sat in the back with Sterling, this time holding his hand and definitely imparting comfort. Occasionally she and Hayden clashed eyes in the mirror, his questioning, hers reassuring. *I'm okay. I'm handling this.*

Duncan was dismayed, not only to be left out of the long journey back home—*Why can't Birdie ride with me? I hate driving alone*—but also befuddled entirely by the decision to commit Sterling. *Because of me? He'll be fine. This is going to pass. He can just hit me again.*

"I will, if you like," Hayden offered, cutting the heavy tension and sadness with what may or may not have been a joke.

It took a long time to check Sterling into the hospital. He looked frightened and alone, so reminiscent of their dad when he was in one of his lulls. "You're doing the right thing," Birdie assured him, holding him close and whispering words of reassurance in his ear. "Dad has never sought help, would never seek help. You're never going to end up like him, not on my watch," she promised, kissing both cheeks. He held her tightly in return a moment, then turned and walked through the doors, where she wasn't allowed to follow.

Hayden held out his hand for her. They walked silently side by side and drove the remainder of the way home, once again in silence. When they arrived, they remained in the car, neither of them making a move to get out, nor a move toward each other. Finally Hayden turned to look at Birdie, and Birdie turned to look at Hayden. A flicker of tension rose between them, strong and potent. Hayden opened his mouth to speak and a car swung in behind them, headlights blaring in the rearview mirror.

Birdie sighed. She knew that car. Duncan emerged and ripped open the passenger door. "We need to talk."

She faced Hayden again with a resigned smile. He brought her hand to his lips and kissed it. She touched her palm to his cheek and allowed Duncan to tug her from the car.

He steamrolled ahead of her, barreling his way onto the front porch. He whirled and faced her. They squared off, staring. She braced herself for his angry blast. He opened his mouth and burst into loud, violent tears, tossing himself onto her shoulder like a toddler who lost his favorite stuffed animal. She staggered under the weight of him but didn't let go, soothing him instead by patting his back and murmuring little shushing noises.

"I never meant…and Sterling is…and you are…both of you…all my fault," he exclaimed in little bits and pieces of near hysteria.

"Shh, shh, shh," she said to him, remembering when Hayden said it to her. So powerful, that little sound. So comforting when said in the right way, with care and kindness.

Eventually his sobbing gave way to little hiccups and shudders, and still he didn't let her go. The weight of him was crushing, but she didn't release her hold. They sank to a sitting position on the porch steps. His arms were still around her, his face pressed to her chest. She ran her hand over his head, over and over, rocking him slightly.

"All I want is you," he murmured. "It's all I've wanted for so long, I don't remember not wanting you. When I think how close I came to losing you." He shuddered.

Birdie froze. "Duncan, we are not together. I can't be with you in that way."

He sat up, scowling now. "Is this about Paxton?"

"No, I told you. He and I are friends. He's working on his own things at the moment."

"Then what is this about? Don't tell me you don't want me, Birdie. I know you do. I could kiss you right now, and you would fall to pieces in my arms. Don't you think I feel it? This thing that bounces between us."

She let him go and put some space between them because he was right; she was weak where he was concerned now. If he reached for her, she would be lost. She would give in, would cling to him, would match him passion for passion.

"Duncan, it's been a long couple of days. I slept two hours. I put my brother in a mental ward." Her voice broke. She took a breath and continued on. "I cannot do this with you right now."

"When?"

"I don't know, but not now. Please."

"All right," he agreed. He stood and used the back of his hand to wipe his nose, exactly as he had done when he was a gross kid who belched and rubbed her face in his sweaty armpit for meanness. "But I am not giving up on us, Birdie Thompson. Hear me?" His index finger jutted at her, menacing in its forcefulness. "We are not through."

She sighed but otherwise didn't reply, remaining curled in a protective ball on the front porch, long after he drove away.

When she finally went inside for the night, she saw *Mend Over Matter* lying open on her desk. She sat and surveyed herself in the mirror. It was time to revise the *you you* she wanted to be.

"I want to be strong enough to handle being alone," she whispered. The last twenty four hours with her brother had been a revelation. She always believed Sterling was the glue holding everybody together. Turned out it was her, and wasn't that a kick in the teeth? How could she possibly support everyone—her mom, her dad, Sterling, Duncan, even Hayden—when she was such a complete and utter mess? *By not being a mess anymore,* she thought.

Step one: stop waiting on a man to come along and save her. Sterling had his own demons. Duncan was a demon. Hayden was dealing with unmerited heartache. Her father had been an emotional no-show since birth.

Step two: figure out her strengths and play to them. Birdie was kind. She was quirky. And apparently she was resilient. That was a new one on her, so perhaps there were others. Time to plumb the hidden depths.

Step three: stop waiting for a better version of herself to really live. How was it possible that she was a travel agent for a living but had never been anywhere? She would find a destination, plan it, and save the money to get there.

She should be exhausted, and she was. But in another way she was exhilarated. Life was not going to make her a victim. Look out, world: Birdie Thompson is ready to live.

First thing first, Birdie went to her closet and began tearing out clothes that didn't fit her new style or personality, basically most of everything she owned. She kept the neon pink workout gear, the dress from her disaster date with Duncan, an emerald colored shirt she usually reserved for St. Patrick's Day, and her two favorite pairs of jeans. She caught sight of her favorite hoodie, a castoff from Duncan from a few years ago with the logo of the college he and Sterling both attended. She picked it up by the tips of her fingers, as if it were a dead rat in need of disposal, but before she could toss it, she laid it on her bed and stared at it, pondering. All that time, all those years, Duncan had been in love with her and she'd had no idea. By their small town community's standards, he was a massive catch, and he'd wanted her, mousy Birdie Thompson. What other surprises might be in store for her? Who else might be lurking on her horizon, waiting to surprise her, to make her see them in a way she never would have guessed?

She folded the shirt and put it back in her drawer. Regardless of the sticky situation with Duncan, they had a long and storied history. He was part of her life, would likely always be part of her life in one way or another. And it was a sublimely comfortable hoodie.

After rearranging what was left of her clothes, she crawled in her bed and curled into a little ball. Even though she was now determined not to depend on a man to fix her life, she missed Hayden and the reassuring pressure of his arm on her waist. Strange how she'd only had it for a few hours, and yet it had felt like it belonged. Before she could talk herself out of it, she reached for her phone and sent him a text.

Status report, and go:

Tired but restless.

Me, too, she agreed.

Also, I miss you.

Me, too, she agreed again.

But, Birdie, I'm so not ready for you. This weekend proved it. Great as it was, the pain is still so raw. I'm impatient for it to be over, to be healed, to be well enough to move on again. But it just keeps coming back around.

Hayden, I know. I feel like you're pressuring yourself for my sake, and you shouldn't. I am doing perfectly fine exactly as is. It may shock you to know I'm working on my own stuff over here.

I know, but I feel like my heart is cleaved in two. Last night, just holding you while you slept, was...it was everything. Like we found a loophole where we could be together with none of the other stuff getting in the way.

You mean the stuff that happens when we're awake?

How is it that we haven't actually talked to each other, and yet I hear you saying that in your voice? You make me laugh, sweet girl. In this world that's worth its weight in gold.

You show up. In my world, that's unprecedented.

Truly, we are amazing. We should probably fall in love and be together forever.

Easy peasy.

I know, right? Like it's hard to find lifelong love and make it last or something, he replied.

I'm going to sleep with my phone on my pillow so it seems like you're here. Don't judge me for being a socially repressed emo teenager, she said.

Don't judge me when you find out I've already been doing that every night, he replied.

She sent him a heart emoji and finally fell asleep.

CHAPTER 26

The next morning Birdie opened Sterling's shop. He hadn't wanted her to at first, until she pointed out that he was still trying to be Mr. Perfect and do everything on his own.

You already work three jobs, he'd argued.

What's one more? Plus I love the shop, she'd replied, and he hadn't been able to deny that fact. Working at his store was a little bit like living her dream vicariously through him. And she was fulfilling a need; financially he couldn't remain closed indefinitely.

She opened on time, and it didn't take long for the curiosity seekers to come calling, asking gentle or downright probing questions about Sterling. Such was the price of living in a small town, there were no secrets. And since everyone bought a little something, Birdie didn't mind. She told them Sterling was taking some time off. They replied with solemn nods, likely guessing the truth. They might not know about Sterling's breakdown, but they knew about Duncan's betrayal and could guess there was a lot of hurt involved. Only a few were intrepid enough to mention Duncan.

"He's family, we're working through it," she replied, a statement that worked on a lot of levels.

In the afternoon, the bell dinged and she looked up to see her dad. Birdie was fairly certain he'd never been in Sterling's shop before. He made no secret of the fact that he didn't approve, that he thought Sterling was settling. She didn't say anything as he meandered the shop, taking it all in. The fact that he was out, shaved and showered, told her he was feeling better. Whether he was in a manic phase, she didn't know, and she braced herself for whatever might emerge when he finally arrived at the desk.

He did so eventually, regarding her with a sweeping glance. "Changed your hair," he noted. She had swept it up and borrowed one of her mother's vintage floral bandeaus. Time to embrace her inner bohemian and make the outside as quirky and eclectic as her interior.

"Only a little," she said, trying not to be defensive. With her father, it was sometimes hard to tell an observation from a criticism. His eyes narrowed.

"Didn't that used to be your mother's?"

She touched the bandeau self-consciously. "Yes."

"I always liked it on her. Made her look like a hippie."

She laughed. Her mother was the most staid and steady person she knew, not given to whimsy or flights of fancy at all. "Yep, that's Mom all right."

He smiled. "She had her moments." He leaned his forearms on the counter. "Did I ever tell you about the time we went backpacking out west?"

"No," she said, tilting her head at him in surprise. "When was that?"

"When we were first married, right before Sterling came along. Believe it or not, it was your mom's idea."

"No way," Birdie said.

He nodded. "She pointed out that we wouldn't have a lot of time for travel and adventure after we had kids, and rightly so."

"Planned spontaneity, that sounds like Mom," Birdie said.

He looked down, picking at a spot on the counter. "I miss her."

"I think she misses you too."

His head snapped up. "Yeah?"

"In some ways."

"Yeah," he said, tone dimming.

The door dinged again. They both turned to see Hayden enter and then pause as if uncertain of his welcome. Birdie gave him a lopsided smile, also uncertain. But it was too late to turn back now. Forcing a smile he walked in and headed toward the back. Her father watched him enter and then turned, tracking his progress through the store.

"He come in here often?" her dad asked. His tone sounded better than last time, less hostile, more neutral.

"Hayden's a big reader, Dad," she hedged. She was certain Hayden had also never been in Sterling's shop before.

Her dad eyed her. "How do you know?"

"We're friends," she said, tone defiant.

"I guess that explains a few things."

There was an awkward few beats where she wondered if he might apologize, and then it occurred to her he was also waiting on her to do the same. After a few seconds, he cleared his throat. "I, uh, heard about Sterling and Chelsea. Or rather Duncan and Chelsea." He blew out a breath. "Man, what a thing." He was taking it better than she might have imagined, and she sighed a little in relief.

"It's hard, but I think they'll pull through it. Apparently it was a drunken mishap on Duncan's part."

Her dad nodded, then took a bracing breath and blurted, "Birdie, where is Sterling?"

She didn't want to tell him, had no idea how to say the words. Telling her mother had been hard enough. She hadn't cried, but she had shut herself in her room for the remainder of the evening, a sure sign she was upset. But if she didn't tell her dad and he found out some other way, he would be livid at being excluded.

"He's at the hospital," she whispered, darting a glance around. It was only Hayden in the store, and he already knew. But in a small town the walls seemed to have ears.

Her dad stared at her, paling slightly. "What? Why? What happened, what's wrong with him?"

"He was having a hard time and needed a bit of help."

"What kind of help?" her dad demanded.

"He was feeling a bit depressed. He's being evaluated to see if he needs medication."

Her dad blinked at her. She wondered if he was seeing himself in Sterling. "What? Why would you let him do that?"

"Why would I not?" Birdie challenged.

"Because now they're going to know, he's going to be in the system. People are going to talk about him."

"People are already talking about him. I don't know who *they* are, but the only system he's going to be in is the hospital's."

"You don't understand, Birdie, you're too young. There's a stigma attached to this kind of thing. He'll never be able to get a job."

She motioned to the space around them. "He's self-employed."

"This can't last forever. He can barely keep it afloat now. And then what? Who's going to hire a crazy guy?"

"See, these are all the things you need to get out of your system before you see him because they are the opposite of helpful and supportive."

"No, you don't know. This is being supportive, this is looking out for him. It's not the same for girls." He motioned to her, condemning her once again for being female. "For men, this kind of thing sticks and follows them around. Women won't have anything to do with him."

"Dad, if women didn't go for guys with mental health issues, half the world wouldn't have been born," Birdie said.

"This is serious, young lady," her father snapped.

"I know it is," she replied, equally as terse. "You weren't there, you don't know. Sterling needed help, might continue to need help for some time. The best thing we can do is love and support him right now. Second guessing him and making him feel bad isn't the way."

Her father geared up to reply but was preempted by Hayden who set a book on the counter between them. Birdie reached for it, glimpsing the title. *Mend Over Matter* stared back at her. She exploded in a combination laugh and cry and leaned over the counter, grasping his shirt and bringing him close enough to kiss both cheeks. Then, swiping her own wet cheeks, she rang him up and placed his book in a bag.

"Mr. Thompson," Hayden said politely, giving him a nod.

Her father nodded in return. "How's your dad, Hayden?"

Birdie, surprised by his polite tone, did her best not to let it show.

"He's well, sir, thank you. And how are you?"

"I'm…I'm alive," her father replied.

"Some days that's the best any of us can hope for." He tossed Birdie a little wink, picked up his bag, and let himself out of the shop.

"Still don't like him," her dad said. "But I'm trying to be nice."

"I appreciate that, Dad. I do. He's a good guy, I promise."

"Well, he seems important to you," her father said, twisting his fingers nervously together.

Birdie blinked at him. She didn't think her father noticed her enough to realize what was important to her, or who. "He is," she said. "And I think Sterling is going to be okay, I really do. He needed a little nudge. We all do sometimes."

Her father sighed. "I suppose."

"Dad, thanks for coming in today. It was nice to see you." With a bit of wonder, she realized she meant it. Nice visits with her father were so few and far between as to be noteworthy.

He smiled. "You're welcome. You should wear that hairband thing more, it looks good on you. You're pretty like your mom." With that he turned and walked away, leaving Birdie gawking after him, wondering what magic brought it all about.

Later that night someone knocked on her door. She opened it, saw no one, and looked down. The entire Blu-Ray series of *Murder She Wrote* sat on her doorstep. Beaming, she picked it up and hugged it to her chest and texted Hayden.

THUS ANSWERING *the question is there such a thing as the perfect gift. Thank you. I love it.*

.   .   .

You're welcome. Quick question: What's a You You?

It took Birdie a long time to answer because she was laughing too hard.

CHAPTER 27

The next day Birdie had to return to her own job so her mom took a turn running Sterling's store. It was her first time doing so, but there weren't many customers and she got through it okay, even enjoyed the change of pace, if her unnatural stream of chatter was to be believed.

On the third day, Birdie went to retrieve Sterling who seemed tired and subdued and possibly a bit chagrined.

"Why do you look like that?" she asked.

"Like what?" he said, tensing.

"Like you're embarrassed to be picked up from the loony bin by your little sister," she said. His façade cracked and he smiled, shaking his head.

"Geez, Birdie, have some sensitivity here."

"Oh, you're right. He-llo, Ster-ling," she said, overly loud, enunciating all the syllables. "My name is Bir-die." She flapped her hands together, mimicking a bird.

Now he was fully laughing. "Can't you even aim for normal?"

"That's a pretty low bar." She grabbed his hand and gave it an excited shake. "I'm so excited to show you all the changes that have come about since you've been away. There's this new restaurant now called McDonalds. I think you're going to love it."

He put her in a headlock and kissed her cheek. "I don't know why I put up with you sometimes. How'd it go at the store? I should probably stop by and check on it today."

"Yeah, about that."

He tensed again and she hastened to continue.

"No, it was great. The first day brought all the gawkers, but they bought stuff. Yesterday mom did fine and it was a normal day of sales and today…"

"Mom can't be running it today, it's not her day off," he said.

"Right," she agreed, nodding.

"And you're here with me," he drawled.

"Man, those Hardy Boys books were not wasted on you."

He picked her up and twirled her around. "Who's running my store, pipsqueak?"

"Hayden."

He blinked at her, holding back his grimace. He wanted to say something negative or nasty, but how could he? Birdie laughed, remembering when Hayden volunteered.

This is so incredibly sweet of you, she'd told him.

I'm doing it for you, but also for Sterling.

Before she could fawn over his selflessness some more, he texted an addendum.

He's going to hate it.

. . .

EVERY TIME she thought about it she giggled, including now, watching the realization play across Sterling's face that he was now beholden to his lifelong arch enemy.

"Man, that guy," he said, shaking his head. "He's diabolical."

"I think you mean adorable," Birdie corrected.

"I think you're the one who's delusional." He plucked his keys from her grasp and held the passenger door for her.

"So how was it, really?" she asked when he slid behind the wheel and adjusted it, frowning because she'd moved his perfectly aligned mirrors.

"After the initial embarrassment and uncertainty, it was kind of restful. I hadn't been sleeping well the last few weeks. They gave me a sedative and I basically spent the first fifteen hours unconscious. Then I woke and ate and slept again. That alone was restorative. I spent a long while talking with the psychiatrist."

He paused to merge into traffic. "And," Birdie prompted.

"She doesn't think I'm bi-polar, but she said it's something to keep an eye on, given Dad's history. She thinks I'm merely depressed and anxious. She put me on a medication and I'm going to see a counselor for follow up."

"Do you feel better?"

"Not yet, but she said it could take a couple of weeks for the medication to kick in and stabilize everything. Plus she pointed out that I am, in fact, in the midst of a stressful and painful situation, so my reaction to it might not be completely overblown."

He gripped the wheel and hunched. She had the sense there was more he wasn't telling her. She poked him. He batted her hand away but continued.

"It's not just the thing with Chelsea and Duncan, though. These are issues I've been dealing with a long time and trying to hide." He darted her a glance. "Trying to be perfect, as your boyfriend would say."

"He's not my boyfriend."

He shook his head, as if no matter her connection to Hayden he would still be puzzled and disgusted by it. He cleared his throat. "She recommended I not be alone right now. And, honestly, my finances aren't doing too great. Would it be okay if I moved back in with you and Mom for a while?"

She rolled her eyes. "Sterling, duh. As if you even have to ask. Home is home."

"If you say 'duh,' you're only a pretend grownup."

"I *am* only a pretend grownup. I'm going to make some changes of my own."

"Anything I can help with?"

She started to say no, then eyed him. "I don't suppose I could convince you to go shopping with me. I got rid of most of my clothes."

"Sure," he said.

"What?" she said, wriggling with excitement. "Would you really?"

"Yes, I'm the one of us who enjoys shopping, remember?"

"Oh, yeah," she said. He and Duncan had always been into their clothes. To Birdie it was one more symptom of their shallowness, but right now it might come in handy. Sterling had always been a better dresser, one more line that separated them into popular and geek for life.

They were already in the city. Sterling diverted to shopping, seemingly glad for the distraction. "I'm not certain exactly what I'm looking for, except I want something that's more me, the real me. No more mousy brown or gray stuff."

"Excellent," Sterling said. "I have some ideas. Put yourself in my capable hands."

Her natural instinct was to argue. Could she actually trust her brother to dress her? Then she realized the answer was yes. Sterling wouldn't make her look bad or outlandish, wouldn't dress her in anything uncomfortable or too flamboyant. "Okay," she agreed, and he darted her a look.

"That went easier than I thought. I expected more argument."

"You're crazy now. I should probably give into you on some stuff."

He snorted a laugh and gave her shoulder a shove. "You're a curse," he said, the warm affection in his tone belying his words.

The day was exhausting, but in a good way. Under Sterling's guidance, Birdie assembled a new and colorful wardrobe, the fact that it was figure flattering and trendy were added bonuses.

"What are you going to do about Chelsea and Duncan?" she asked when they were once again on their way home.

"Chelsea and I are over, it's a done deal. And if I'm being honest, we were having problems for a long time. I hid a lot from her because I didn't want her to know how much I was struggling. She was impatient and frustrated with that, maybe rightly so, maybe not. In any case, I'm not certain the thing with Duncan was wholly unplanned on her part. She knew he was going to that party that night. As for Duncan, I don't know. I can't imagine how I could ever forgive him for this."

"But also you can't imagine how you could ever not," she said.

He nodded.

"We're lifers, Sterling. It's a blessing and a curse. Maybe it's because of Mom and Dad. Seeing the way she hung in there, no matter what, even when things were so hard, she still loved him."

"Good news for me. Maybe someday there will be some girl willing to go along with my particular menu of mental illness," he said, his tone somewhere between upbeat and self-deprecating.

"There will," Birdie declared. "Look at you, you're a catch. A handsome and kind business owner. You're like a Hallmark movie waiting to happen."

He snorted a laugh. "Newsflash, little sister, guys don't want to be a Hallmark movie."

"What do you want to be?" she asked.

"Tom Brady, maybe."

She laughed. "Way to keep the goals attainable."

"What's the big deal? All I need to do is win a few Super Bowls and marry an international super model."

"Say super one more time in that sentence, I dare you," she said, poking him.

"Super," he returned, poking her.

They drove to her house. Birdie shouldn't have been surprised to see Duncan waiting on the porch for them, but she still was. He sat on the steps looking lonely and forlorn.

"I'm not sure I'm up for this," Sterling murmured.

"Want me to distract him? Fair warning, the only weapon in my arsenal seems to be intense makeout sessions."

"I am going to puke," Sterling returned, giving her shoulder a shove.

"I might, too, if I have to kiss him again," she said and they high fived.

"How is he?" Duncan asked at their approach. "I mean, how are you...how is stuff?"

"Don't say stuff," Birdie warned. "It's one of his trigger words. Also, we're not allowed to show him mirrors or pictures of anything with a monkey on it. And if he starts clucking like a chicken, cover all the outlets and knives."

Sterling laughed and bypassed them, going inside without a word to Duncan who picked Birdie up and tossed her over his shoulder, smacking her hard on the bottom.

"And one to grow on," he said.

"Not my birthday," she said, squirming to be set down.

"Maybe it's mine," he said, setting her down too close in front of him. She took a step back and sat down, patting the step beside her.

He sank into it with a sigh. "How is he, really?"

"Humble, ready and willing to make some important changes, I think."

"Do you think he and Chelsea will stay together?"

"No." She turned to survey him. "Do you think *you* and Chelsea will stay together?"

He grimaced. "No. Mainly because we were never together to begin with. I hate to think of them breaking up because of me, if he really loved her. And, I don't know, he'd be a really good stepdad to my kid. It would be nice to keep it all in the family that way." He rested his chin on his knees and turned to look at her when she gave a rueful little chuckle. "What?"

"I'm trying to imagine what the pictures in your head look like. In what universe would Sterling be content to sit back and be stepdad to the child you fathered with his girlfriend?"

"It would solve a lot of problems," Duncan said.

"A lot of your problems, maybe," she said.

"Exactly." He gave a definitive nod.

"Duncan, you are so messed up," she murmured, pressing her thumb to her forehead.

He opened his mouth and closed it. "Maybe," he conceded after a few beats. "I notice your boy toy isn't here today to touch you adoringly."

"That's because he spent the day working at Sterling's store."

He sat up. "What? Why would you let him do that?"

"I didn't let him. He volunteered, to be nice. That's the kind of guy he is, like his dad. A helper."

"Helper monkey, more like."

She jabbed him in the solar plexus and he oofed.

"I would have done it," he said mutinously, rubbing his middle.

"I contemplated it, but then I was afraid maybe you'd go to some other bookstore and get it pregnant," she said.

He shook his head. "Birdie, I swear."

"I don't think Sterling is there yet, ready to have you that much in his grill."

"And you?" he faced her. "Are you ready to have me that much in your grill?"

He was very close, close enough to smell. Somehow over the last few weeks, he'd become even more attractive, at least to her. She noted now the way his hair curled at the temples when it became sweaty, the way his eyes crinkled at the corners when he was amused by her. All she had to do was tilt her head in invitation and they'd be kissing. And the kissing would be good, intense and bone melting. "No." She inched away, gaining some distance.

Duncan sighed and hunched forward again. "What do I have to do to get you there?"

"You can't."

"Don't say that."

"It's true, and it's not anger talking. You can't undo what's been done."

"I don't understand this. I know you're mad for Sterling's sake, and I know it was a bad thing I did to him. But I didn't do it to you; I didn't cheat on you. Our relationship is separate from my relationship with him."

"I'm not certain it is, but that's not why."

"Then why?" He sounded so sad, so devoid of his usual Duncan cockiness.

"I haven't found the words to articulate it yet. I'm still trying. But when I do, I'll try to explain it. Right now, I need you to respect my decision. We are friends. Don't pursue me."

"Why do you always feel like you have to find the right words for everything? Just tell me and put me out of my misery."

"If I don't find the right words, I'll mess it up and extend both our misery. Why can't you ever give me time and space when I need it?"

"Because I hate it. Because any space between us makes me feel panicky, like a chasm is going to open up and take you away from me. And I don't think I can function without you, Birdie." His voice broke and he expelled a hot blast of air, sucking it back in again and trying to regain his equilibrium.

"I'm still right here, Duncan."

He shook his head furiously like an angry toddler. "It's not the same. Why do you think I bought the farm? I know how much you love it. I don't want to be there without you, without us together."

"You put that on me, but you never said a word, never hinted at a future for us, never gave me any clue you had feelings or were making plans."

"How could you not have known, and how could you not have felt the same way?" he exploded, tossing his arms up.

"Stop," she said, becoming irritated. "Your feelings are not my feelings, and I am not responsible for them. And I just love how you're making yourself the victim here when, darlin', check a mirror, you're the villain."

Far from being insulted by the barb, he grinned. "Yes, but, *darlin'*, villains have all the fun." He leaned forward and kissed her, a light peck, before she could protest, then jogged toward his car while she looked for something to toss at him. She picked up a rock and threw it hard, missing him by a mile, then threw another when his laughter echoed through the night.

CHAPTER 28

Two nights later, Birdie made supper for her mom and Sterling and invited both Duncan and Hayden.

"Why don't you add Chelsea and Dad in there, really extend the misery for all of us," Sterling suggested, pinching a deviled egg while she wasn't looking.

"Keep getting in the way while I'm trying to work, and maybe I will," Birdie returned, annoyed to keep tripping over him in the tiny kitchen.

"Seriously, why are you punishing me this way?" he asked. "Minus the good food. Did you make sweet tea?"

He looked so earnest and adorable she had to pause and ruffle his hair. "Yes, I made sweet tea. And I am not punishing you. I'm trying to help you along. You and Duncan need to spend time together, to get back on track. This is a neutral setting and y'all won't fight with Mom here."

"And Hayden?"

"Will be here for me."

"How come you blather on about how much you like this guy and I've never seen you once talk to each other?" he asked.

"It's our thing," she said. "You couldn't possibly begin to understand it. I'm way too deep and complex for you."

"That's for certain. If he can delve into that psyche, good luck to him. I should warn him to bring a tow rope and reading material."

"He never lacks for reading material."

"What does he read?" Sterling asked, eyeing her critically. He was judgmental about the things people read, a job hazard of owning a bookstore.

"Mostly *Curious George,* but he's trying to work his way up to *Clifford.*"

"I might be starting to feel sorry for him," Sterling muttered, stealing another egg.

"Touch those eggs again, and you're going to be the one in need of help," Birdie yelled, jabbing her spatula at him.

"Looks like I'm in time for the brawl," Duncan said. He entered the kitchen after letting himself in uninvited, as usual. There was some comfort in that, she supposed. She whirled her spatula on him.

"No, actually, I was saying what someone should have said to you in regards to Chelsea a few months ago."

His jaw dropped and Sterling guffawed. "Birdie, I swear." He lunged for the spatula, intending to swat her with it, she knew. She dodged him and backstepped until she was flush against the counter behind her. Duncan advanced, pressing his body to hers and wagging his brows. She maintained her grip of the spatula, holding it between them like a gun. A knock sounded on the door.

"That's Hayden," she said, breathless from Duncan's proximity. "Y'all act like you've got some sense tonight." With effort, she wriggled away from Duncan, ducking beneath his arm to return her attention to the chicken she was frying. "Sterling, get the door please. I can't let my chicken burn."

"Let that chicken burn, baby, you know you want to," Duncan said, circling her neck from behind and leaning in to kiss her cheek.

"Weird, Duncan. So weird," she said, attempting to shake him off.

"Birdie, can you pretty please forgive me and move on? You know you want to. You always do. It's our thing." He nuzzled his nose against her ear. She knew he was doing it merely so Hayden would see when he entered, which he did only thirty seconds later, and it was why she waited to speak.

"I swear, you are taking your life in your hands while I have access to hot oil. Get off."

She held the spatula aloft again, but this time he heeded the warning, hands up in full meekness. "Whatever you say, *darlin'*."

She tossed Hayden an exasperated smile, rolling her eyes. He smiled in return, shaking his head.

"This is so weird," Sterling mused, watching them. "I'm honestly not sure which of you is responsible, Birdie because she's always been a sweetheart oddball or Paxton because he's always been singular."

"My money's on Birdie," Duncan added. "This has her fingerprints all over it."

"You're right," Birdie agreed sweetly. "Let's you and I institute a similar no-talking rule. You start."

Hayden chortled.

"Are you allowed to talk to us?" Sterling asked him.

"If I have somethin' to say," Hayden returned.

"Well, then, thank you for watching my store. I really appreciate it," Sterling said, the words wrenched from somewhere deep and painful.

"It was no skin off my nose," Hayden said, nodding his thanks as Birdie poured him a glass of sweet tea unbidden. "Maybe we could knock down that wall between our shops, make a giant repair-based bookstore."

"Well, I'm pretty sure I'd need a whole lot more therapy for that," Sterling said and a bit of the ever-present tension eased from between the two men. Duncan scowled, picking up the mantel. He had always been jealous of Sterling's friendships with other people, even Birdie, and he definitely didn't want him to relax his I-hate-you stance on Hayden.

"He's allowed to play with other people," Birdie told him, handing him a glass of tea as well.

"But you're not," Duncan said, giving her a heated stare over his glass.

"Man, you are trying your best to make this night into a Mexican soap opera, aren't you?" Hayden asked, earning another laugh from Sterling.

"I don't have to force it, seeing as how I'm the only one in this room who's actually kissed her," Duncan said.

"Don't look at me, I sure haven't," Sterling inserted.

"It's okay. I have a feeling when all is said and done, I'll be the last one to kiss her," Hayden added, steady gaze settling on Duncan who returned it with a glare.

The front door opened, announcing their mother's arrival from work. "Mama, come save me from the testosterone. I'm drowning in it," Birdie called.

Her mother breezed into the room, giving hugs to Sterling and Duncan and holding out her hand to Hayden. Sterling gave the introduction and they made polite chatter while Birdie finished dinner.

"Oh, my lands, this is why people have children, so they can come home to supper on the table," her mother said, beaming at her full plate of food. She said the blessing and everyone started to eat. "Now, Hayden, I know everything there is to know about everyone here but you. What can you tell me about yourself, besides what Birdie's already told me?"

"I might be more interested to hear what Birdie's had to say, ma'am," he said, smiling gaze shifting to Birdie. She regarded him with flushed cheeks and slid another deviled egg onto his plate.

"Not a lot, if I'm being honest. Birdie keeps her cards close. I'd fault her, but she doubtless learned it from me. So far I know you used to be a fireman and you took over your father's business after coming back home."

"That's about it. I was married for three years and it ended rather abruptly."

"Divorce is hard, no matter how long the marriage. It's like a death, I think, and requires full grief. But I'm living proof there is life after." She smiled a little secret smile and Birdie and Sterling shot each other a look.

"Mom, are you trying to tell us you're seeing someone?" Sterling asked, working hard not to grimace.

"You never know," their mother replied.

Birdie turned to Duncan. "Please don't tell us you got to Mom, too."

Both Duncan and her mother choked, him with mortification and her with laughter. "Birdie, I swear," he said when he could rightly breathe again. "I'm sorry, Mrs. Thompson, although you're the one who raised her, so rightly you should probably apologize for foisting her on us in this condition."

"Yes, but what would we do without our Birdie?" Mrs. Thompson replied, sopping sweet tea off her shirt.

"Hear, hear," Sterling seconded, lifting his glass. Hayden and then Duncan followed suit.

"Y'all quit," Birdie said, blushing.

Sterling's phone buzzed with a text, and he held it aloft to read. "Oh, hey, Dunc, it's your mistress. 'I miss you. Can we talk.' Want me to pass anything along when I tell her to drop dead?"

"She's not my mistress. I told you I don't even like her," Duncan argued.

"You must have liked her for a minute, or at least parts of her," Birdie interjected.

Duncan rounded on her. "I wish you would stay out of this."

"I wish you had never dragged me into it," Birdie returned.

"What was the best part of everyone's day?" their mother asked.

Birdie and Sterling shot each other guilty glances. It was the same thing she used to do to try and diffuse tension when they were smaller and their dad's moods hung heavy.

"Sweet tea and fried chicken," Sterling said meekly, tucking his phone away.

"Being here with family," Duncan said purposefully.

"This meal for certain," Hayden agreed.

"Same for me. What about you, Birdie?" her mother asked.

"Birdie's hasn't happened yet," Duncan said with an over exaggerated leer and nudge. "That's for later, when she walks me outside."

"Sterling, give Duncan some of your medication. He's having delusions," Birdie said. Everyone laughed, and the heavy tension was broken. The remainder of the meal was light and fun. Hayden talked, though not directly to Birdie. They caught fleeting eye contact, and each time she felt a fluttering little certainty in her chest. *He belongs here. He fits.* Somehow her brother's enemy was becoming a friend to them all. Well, maybe not Duncan. There was still no love lost there.

They cleared the plates. Birdie said she would wash them later, but her mother volunteered. "The cook gets the rest of the night off, and you know I enjoy washing dishes."

The four younger people turned toward the living room. Birdie tucked her arm companionably through Hayden's. He gave it a squeeze and patted her hand. Duncan watched them with a calculating gleam.

"Birdie, I need to talk to you outside."

"What an excellent statement, Duncan. Next week we'll work on question marks," Birdie replied.

He sighed, longsuffering. "Birdie, may I please talk to you outside?"

"Just talk?" she asked.

"Just talk," he affirmed.

"No," she replied, and continued on her way.

"Confound it, woman," Duncan said and picked her up, dragging her away from Hayden with one arm tucked around her waist.

Hayden watched her go, eyebrows raised in question. *Rescue?*

She shook her head, rolling her eyes. It was best to let him speak his piece and get it over with. They reached the porch and he set her down in front of him close, too close. Birdie took a step back.

"What is it?" she asked because he looked like he actually was about to burst with information of some sort and not a sneak attack of kisses like usual lately.

"I need to say something, and I want you to know I'm saying it as a friend and not as someone you're in a relationship with."

"That's good because you're not someone I'm in a relationship with," she said.

Ignoring her, he pressed on. "You don't have a lot experience with men."

"Good talk," she said, pushing away from the wall to go back inside.

"Would you just," he put out a hand, anchoring her in place. "Please, this is important."

"Fine. Carry on."

"You haven't ever been in a real relationship before," he said.

She frowned. "I dated Peter Quigley in high school." She and Peter had gone to prom together and had a few lackluster dates and kisses. He wasn't the love of her life, but she'd liked him. It had hurt when he abruptly stopped calling with no explanation.

"Peter Quigley is not the name of someone you date. Peter Quigley is the name of the character who gets killed in the first five minutes of a horror movie. And I know exactly what you did and didn't do with Peter Quigley."

"How do you know?" she asked, squinting up at him.

"Because I twisted his arm and pressed his face into the wall until he told me," he said.

"Is that why he stopped calling me?"

He shrugged, smiling.

She rubbed her temples. How many men had Duncan scared away from her? What if she'd somehow been secretly popular and he kept beating everyone away? Unlikely, but still. "You had no right."

"Of course I did. You were like my little sister."

She grimaced. "That puts a whole new and disturbing spin on why you started making out with me."

He gave his trademark Birdie-is-making-me-crazy sigh. "The point is that unlike you, I have had a lot of experience with women. I mean a lot." He ended on a smile, wincing when she kicked his shin. "Right, I'll get to it. I'm telling you this because I realize more than you do that what you have with Paxton is a nothing burger."

"A nothing burger?" she repeated, trying not to laugh. "What on earth is a nothing burger?"

"It's a passionless quasi-friendship shared by two people who have never even spoken, let alone kissed," he said.

She scowled. "How do you know we've never kissed? Did you twist his arm? Why don't you go try it? I'll wait." She crossed her arms. Hayden was a good match for Duncan's impressive bulk, and he'd been a firefighter. Somehow in a fist-to-fist match, she thought Hayden would win. And she thought Duncan knew it, too, which was why he never pressed things too far. Duncan hated to lose, and he therefore didn't usually enter the fray if he thought it might be a possibility. It was the same reason he would play ping pong, pool, or poker with Birdie but not Trivial Pursuit.

"I know because I can tell. I'm certain it's flattering when a new guy shows up and starts paying you a bit of attention, and it seems like he's been nice enough to you, so I'm willing to overlook that attention. But the fact remains there is absolutely nothing between the two of you." He took a small step forward. Birdie took one back and bumped the wall. "Not like us. We go back a long way, all the way. Nearly three decades of history together. All the memories we've shared. Girl, you've seen me naked."

"That was an accident," she whispered, hands clutching the bricks behind her for support.

"So you say. But in all the many, many women I've dated, it has never been as combustible as it is with you." He put his hand out and she flinched, but he merely touched his thumb to her belly button, rubbing in a little circle. It was enough, though, and Birdie started to feel weak-kneed and woozy. "One look, one touch, one kiss, and you go up in flames. And so do I. And if you think that's something that comes along more than once in a lifetime, you're crazier than I think you are." He dropped his hand and took a step back, assessing the limp way she leaned against the house for support. "Goodnight, Birdie. Thanks for supper." With a sweet little smile, he turned and walked to his car.

Birdie remained on the porch, sucking oxygen, wishing for a cool breeze for clarity instead of the muggy Georgia humidity. It was like trying to breathe through a wet blanket. Her phone buzzed, startling her.

OKAY OUT THERE? Hayden asked. *The talking stopped.*

WHAT IF WE don't have chemistry? she text blurted.

WHY WOULD YOU SAY THAT? No, never mind, I already know. First, do not let him get in your head. It's what he wants more than anything. He's like Voldemort. Don't say his name out loud, and don't give him the satisfaction of knowing what goes on in your mind. Second, there are different kinds of chemistry, different ways in which people click. You and I, we're simpatico. Our wavelengths and hearts and minds all match. How many people can say that? Third,

THE TEXT ENDED. She stared at her phone, waiting. The door beside her creaked open, and Hayden stepped out. He still held half a glass of sweaty sweet tea. He held it out to her. She shook her head. Eyes on her, he drained it and then reached to set it aside on the wicker stand. He straightened and studied her. They were close enough to brush each other but not pressed together. He took a tiny step closer and reached for her hands, twining all of their fingers together. Birdie stared up at him with big eyes, heart thumping. He smiled down at her, a sweet, affectionate smile. Her heart sank a little because it was so unlike the way Duncan smiled at her before he kissed her. His was so…predatory. But Hayden looked at her like she was an adorable kitten.

He brushed his nose against hers and she found herself tipping instinctively toward him. Their lips touched. He kissed her lightly and pulled away. Then kissed her bottom lip in the same manner, gently. Birdie let go of one of his hands and clutched his shirt, urging him closer. He responded by cupping her neck, deepening the kiss, and then it was as if a dam broke and they were a full-throttle tangle of mouths and arms and hands.

Birdie realized Duncan was correct about one thing: it was different than it was with him. Kissing Duncan was like being scrubbed all over with a pinecone, almost painful in its intensity, an explosion of nerve endings that resulted in somewhat angry kisses. Kissing him was like a metaphor for their entire relationship as they each tried to one up each other on the passion and intensity.

Kissing Hayden felt like someone put a fishhook in her soul and gave it a yank toward him. It was intense and dizzying, almost scary for its depth. But even so she felt safe, as if Hayden was always mindful of her wellbeing, as if taking care of her outweighed getting what he wanted from her. Different from Duncan? Exponentially. Less potent? Not by a country mile.

She had no idea how long they stood there kissing. Eventually Sterling opened the door, poked his head out, and had instant regrets. "Going to need to up my dose," he muttered, retreating back inside.

Hayden let her go, resting his forehead on hers, trying to get a breath. She clutched his shirt in both hands trying to do the same. At last when he could breathe, he offered her a smile. She gave him one in return. He kissed her cheek and jogged to his car. Her phone buzzed a minute later.

THANK YOU FOR SUPPER. It was amazing, like its maker, followed by four fire emojis.

JESSICA AND SETH 4EVER, she replied and smiled, imagining him laughing.

CHAPTER 29

The next morning at work, Birdie opened an email and froze. As a travel agent, she received regular correspondence from cruise lines. Usually she skimmed and disregarded everything, but today one particular notice caught her attention, a job posting. She clicked on it, heart pounding. It sounded like her dream, with time off to explore. But how could she leave everything and everyone here? On the other hand, what did it hurt to apply? She updated her resume, typed a cover letter, and sent them before she could change her mind. Probably nothing would come of it, but she had been brave. Her *you you* was practically humming with pride.

She hadn't heard from Hayden that morning. Thinking of the job made her think of him, so she texted.

THE TEXT BUBBLE disappeared a few times, as it usually did when he had something major to impart or when he needed to say something he didn't want to say. Birdie was working when it finally came through.

My dad died.

She jumped up, clutching her phone. Shelley eyed her with a smile, probably expecting another performance. "Birdie, honey, everything okay?"

"Harry Paxton died," Birdie muttered.

"What?" Shelley exclaimed. "Oh, no."

"Shelley, I'm so sorry, but I have to go. Hayden..." she trailed off. She hadn't told Shelley anything about Hayden. How could she possibly explain that she needed to leave work to be with their next door shop neighbor she had seemingly never spoken to?

"I understand, sweetheart. You go, and you tell him how awful sorry I am, okay?"

Nodding, Birdie dodged forth and hugged her before hastily gathering her things and running out the door. Instinctively she knew Hayden would be at his father's house. She headed there and knocked but no one answered. She tried the door, found it unlocked, and let herself in. Hayden sat on the couch, dazed, a pile of official-looking papers around him. She sank to the couch next to him. He flinched, blinked at her in shock a few seconds, and then burst into wrenching sobs, propelling himself at her.

She gathered him close, kissing his forehead as she ran her hands soothingly over his head. She cried a little, too. For Harry, for the sadness death always brings, but mostly for Hayden. How awful to lose a father, and one as beloved as Harry must hurt even more somehow. Or maybe not. Maybe losing a parent is so painful there is no threshold to compare, no scale based on how well he was liked by everybody else.

He cried himself out and they shifted slightly, reclining so his head was pillowed on her chest. Birdie rubbed his back and felt a little of the tension drain out of him. She wondered if he'd been dreading having to do everything alone and hoped somehow he realized he didn't have to.

The doorbell rang. Hayden made no move to answer it. Birdie started to get up. He gave her a desperate little tug, as if frightened she would disappear. She kissed the top of his head and eased away.

The funeral director stood on the other side of the door, his dark business suit stark contrast to Birdie's bright magenta dress.

"Morning, Mrs. Paxton, I'm Bill Curtis with Curtis, Wright and Roe. I'm awfully sorry for your loss, ma'am. I'm here to finalize arrangements, if now is a good time?"

It wasn't a good time, but since it would likely never be a good time, she moved aside. "Please come in. I'm not Mrs. Paxton, I'm Birdie Thompson, a friend of Hayden's. He's right in here, if you'll follow me."

"Excuse me, ma'am," he said, wiping his feet as he followed her inside. "Are you any relation to Sterling Thompson?"

"Yes, sir, he's my brother."

"Ah, good boy, Sterling."

"Yes, sir, the best," Birdie repeated the old phrase, smiling. Sterling was known and beloved the town over. Most people were surprised to hear he even had a sister. Strangely, the thought no longer hurt. Birdie might fly under the radar, but she had her own life, and it was a good one.

Hayden sat up and shook hands with Mr. Curtis. Birdie stood by, uncertain, feeling suddenly like an intruder. But his eyes turned pleadingly on her and he patted the couch beside him. She sat and clasped his hand, giving it a reassuring squeeze as the two men talked over funeral arrangements. After Harry's last stroke, he wrote out his will, along with instructions for burial, making it as easy as possible on his lone son who had merely to hand Mr. Curtis the instructions, along with a check. Still, it was wrenching. Hayden seemed like a husk of the person who had kissed her last night. How much pain could a person take in a short amount of time? First his divorce and now his father's death. Life wasn't fair sometimes.

The doorbell rang again. Birdie stood to answer it and received a casserole from one of the neighbors who regarded her curiously.

"I'm Birdie Thompson, a friend of Hayden's," she explained. "Thank you so much for your kindness, I'm sure he'll appreciate it."

"Well, you tell him we loved Harry," the woman instructed, eyeing Birdie with suspicion.

"Yes, ma'am," Birdie nodded meekly.

After that four more neighbors arrived, and then five people from the church. Birdie answered the door each time, leaving Hayden in a grief-stricken daze on the couch. She arranged the casseroles in the freezer, shifting them each time to make room for another.

When it was finally time for supper, Birdie heated one of the casseroles. Hayden appeared in the door, either because he smelled food or he missed Birdie's hovering presence. When he eased forward, took her in his arms, and kissed her, she thought it was the latter. She stood on her toes, kissing him in return, trying to imbue all the comfort and care in the world into that kiss. The timer on the microwave dinged and he stepped away from her, breathless and flushed, tears in his eyes. She thought maybe she succeeded in conveying something.

They ate in companionable silence, free hands clasped between them. Birdie wondered if it was ridiculous not to talk to each other at this point. There must be things he wanted to say, emotions he wanted to express. But she also felt like she was following his lead. If he wanted to talk, he would talk. Knowing how much he enjoyed his downtime and the ability to read in peace, she figured he probably found the quiet lack of chatter soothing. Birdie did too, if she were being honest.

After supper they returned to the living room. Hayden lay down, using her lap as a pillow. His conversation with the funeral director let her know Harry's stroke happened around midnight. He was able to call an ambulance and then died before they arrived. The emergency room called Hayden at one, and he'd been up all night. She sifted her fingers through his hair and soon realized he was asleep.

Slowly, she eased out from under him and tiptoed to her purse, searching for a piece of paper and pen.

RAN HOME TO gather some things, but I'll be back. Unless you'd rather I don't return. If you want to be alone, text me and tell me to stay. I'll understand, no hurt feelings. Otherwise I'll bring my things and prepare to stay here the next few days or as long as you need me. XO, B.

SHE EASED out the door and drove home, pausing in the living room to touch base with Sterling and her mother. Sterling, good guy he was, volunteered to do whatever was necessary to help. He felt he owed Hayden, but it was more than that. Sterling was the sort of person who would help anyone, even his oldest enemy. And Hayden was like that, too, she realized. He'd proved it over and over since his return.

She had just finished packing her bag when her phone buzzed.

COME BACK. Need you forever.

SHE LET herself in again and found Hayden still on the couch, looking sad and bereft. He lifted his head to survey her and held out his arm. She scooted under it, curling into his embrace, big spoon to little spoon. She pulled the afghan up to cover them, he kissed her cheek, and a few minutes later they both fell asleep.

CHAPTER 30

Birdie wasn't certain where her place would be, in the combined viewing and funeral, but Hayden kept her by his side, hand firmly in his grasp. No other family came forward to take over his care or offer comfort, and Birdie didn't know it was possible to be so alone. Harry had migrated to their town from North Carolina when he was young, bringing his bride with him. They had Hayden late in life, after being told they would never have children. Hayden's mother died six years ago, right before Harry's first stroke. Every time she thought of how alone he was, she sent him a smile of support, of care and understanding. She sent him a lot of smiles.

Late in the viewing, nearly in time for the funeral to begin, Hayden tensed beside her. She looked up to see what caused it and saw a pretty woman and handsome man making their way forward. Hayden's hand gripped hers with Herculean strength, almost but not quite making her wince.

"Hayden, I'm so sorry," the woman said, reaching forward to hug him. Hayden returned it awkwardly, patting her back a couple of times and quickly breaking away.

"Thank you, and thank you for being here." He slid his arm around

Birdie's shoulders and gave them a squeeze. "This is my…This is my Birdie. This is Kaylee and this is Bryce."

Ah, the ex and the cheating best friend. Birdie wanted to punch them, both of them, for the pain they'd inflicted on Hayden. On the other hand, they were here, showed up in his hour of need. She pasted on what she hoped was a convincingly gracious smile and extended her hand. "How very nice to meet you both. Thank you for being here, it's so kind you came." Hayden gave her shoulder a squeeze, the ghost of a smile on his lips, as if he knew and understood how much effort the words cost her when what she really wanted to do was jab each of them in the solar plexus while their hands were extended.

"Thank you," Kaylee said, eyes lowered slightly in a perplexed frown as her gaze flicked between Hayden and Birdie. Maybe she was being paranoid, but Birdie felt like Kaylee was waiting for her to lower her gaze in either shame or defeat. Instead she notched her chin up slightly, smile widening as her own eyes narrowed.

You tossed him away. To the victor go the spoils.

They took their seats, and it was time for the funeral to begin. Hayden threaded his fingers through hers and led her to the pew. The pastor spoke and opened the floor to anyone from the community who wanted to say a word. A lot of people did. Harry had been friendly and kind, an active member of the community, their beloved handyman and Mr. Fixit. To Birdie's own shock, she found herself slipping from the pew and striding to the front of the room. Despite how much she loathed public speaking, some things were more important than her fear.

"One time when I was little, Harry came to our house to fix our washer. It was a decrepit old thing that broke down approximately once a quarter, usually coinciding with spring rains that made my brother's uniforms their muddiest and stinkiest. I remember my mom saying after one such visit that Harry was the only one who could coax the thing back to life again, that he was an appliance whisperer, some kind of magician. And for a lot of years I believed that was true because, you see, while he was at our house, I cried because my musical jewelry box broke. The little ballerina snapped off and the music refused to play. The box had been my grandmother's and to me it was a precious family heirloom, even though it was likely a cheap piece of junk. Harry took my music box back to his shop and returned it three days later, good as new. The little ballerina spun, the music played. He even managed to fix the wobbly hinge. When I was a kid, a lot of things in my life broke and remained broken. To have someone who took the time to fix one of them actually was magical. Hayden once told me his father was the keeper of lost things and of the old ways of doing things. So it feels like a double loss, not only of a man who was kind and compassionate, but one who understood that fixing things sometimes entailed more than using a screwdriver and wrench. Sometimes it was hearts that needed to be mended, and Harry was never too busy for that, even the heart of a little girl who was often invisible. I'm thankful I knew him." She gave a tremulous little smile and eased off the stage, resuming her place beside Hayden who hugged her, crying.

She rode with him in the processional, stood by him at the graveside, made him a plate at the after-funeral church dinner, and then drove him home again.

Once there, she marched him toward his bedroom, pushed him into bed, and perched on the edge, smoothing his hair off his face. He grasped her hand, tucking it against his face as he fell asleep.

When she was assured he was fully asleep, she stole around gathering her things and went home, sensing he was finally ready to be alone with his grief.

Three days later she received a letter, tucked in her mailbox without a stamp, hand delivered. Sensing it was monumental somehow, she took it to her room before opening it.

DEAR BIRDIE,

THANK you so much for sticking by my side after my father's death. For answering the door and organizing the casseroles, for holding my hand and kissing my head and tucking me in bed at night. For making certain I ate and drank and functioned. For standing by me at the funeral, and especially for the kind words regarding my father.

I've always been a loner, maybe because I've always been alone. In any case, I was never that person who thought I needed anyone, but it turns out I was wrong because I needed you, and you have been the best friend I've ever had. For the last few months I've felt like we're barreling headlong toward something. I've been expectant, almost excited, wishing and hoping to get over my heartache so I could move on with you.

But seeing Kaylee and Bryce at the funeral was... It felt like I successfully dragged myself up ten flights of stairs on two broken legs, only to get kicked down an empty elevator shaft. And I can't in good conscience ask you to keep waiting for me when I don't know if I'll ever be ready.

So I'm asking you, for your sake, to move on from the waiting. Maybe I'm flattering myself that you ever were. You've had Duncan in the background, and while I think you can do ten thousand times better, I no longer have the right to say so because I'm taking myself out of the running.

I figured out something else that's been bugging me since we started talking. You are not a comma, Birdie Thompson. You're the semicolon, the thing that spans the gap and joins all the parts together and keeps them that way. You're vital and important and I love you, so much, you can't know how much you mean to me. The whole world and then some.

I'm sorry I'm too scared and broken for anything more.

Yours, Hayden.

"What's that face for?" Duncan stood in her open doorway, studying her, head tipped in concern.

"Nothing," she said, stuffing the letter back in its envelope and placing it on her nightstand. "What are you doing here?"

"Sterling and I are going to play some one on one."

"Really?" she said, perking up.

"Yes. Apparently if we keep our relationship on the level of sports, he can take out his aggression on the court instead of on my face like he wants to," Duncan said.

"Maybe you and I should play some one on one," Birdie joked.

He laughed, entered uninvited and perched beside her on the bed. His shoulder lightly bumped hers. "Missed you, Stranger."

"I missed you, too," she said sincerely. He reached for her, but she eased away. "I think I found my words."

He eased back, face creasing into a frown. "I'm listening."

"You pursued me hard, knowing you'd gotten another woman pregnant, my brother's girlfriend, no less. I want you to explain your timing on that decision."

"When I found out Chelsea was pregnant, it shook me to my foundation. And my foundation is Sterling and you. I knew things were about to hit the fan in a major way, and I wanted you beside me. I wanted us to be firmly established in a relationship before everything came out."

She studied him a few beats while he tried not to squirm. She thought maybe he sensed the wrongness of his thinking but couldn't articulate what was so bad about it. "If you and I hadn't had our little thing, I would have been mad when I learned about Chelsea. I probably would have kicked you, possibly in the face. But I would have gotten over it and moved on, just like we're all getting over it and moving on now. But instead you made me care about you, made me see you in a whole different way, made me understand what it felt like to kiss you, to want you, to be part of you."

He nodded enthusiastically, mistaking her meaning entirely.

"But, Duncan, how could you do that to me? Do you not understand how completely selfish that was? You dragged me into a love quadrangle with my brother. Did you not think for one second how it would feel to hear you'd impregnated another girl, Sterling's girlfriend, while I sat in your lap, kissing your face? You filled my heart with promises and endearments, and then you lanced it open, for no other reason than because you wanted to have me."

"I didn't mean it like that, Birdie. I got a little desperate. I wasn't thinking, was all. I just knew I couldn't lose you." His Adam's apple bobbed convulsively.

"That's the thing, though. *You* knew that *you* couldn't lose. You gave no thought to me, to my feelings, to the possible repercussions and wounds you would cause me." She took a breath and forced herself to say the next part. "I spent my entire childhood with a selfish man who thought only of his own feelings, his own needs, his own wants, and it eviscerated me. I will not spend the rest of my life the same way. I couldn't fix him. I won't try to fix you." As soon as Birdie made the connection between her dad and Duncan, the mutual self-centeredness, it was impossible not to stop overlaying them in her mind. Tempting as Duncan was to her in some ways, she was resolute; her adulthood would not be a repeat of her unhealthy childhood.

He sniffled and swiped at his nose. "I love you, and I know you love me."

"I really, really believe I do. But sometimes love isn't enough. I won't waste away, losing myself, dying inside, to try and make it so. And I hope you will take this and use it to grow, to fix whatever's going wrong inside you. Because I caught a glimpse of the man you can be, and it's pretty fantastic, knocked me right off my feet. But for self-preservation, I can't wait and hope for the possibility that you might one day turn into him."

"So, what, you're gonna go ride off into the sunset with Paxton now?" he said, tone turning bitter.

"No. I'm gonna ride off into the sunset by myself."

"What are you talking about, Birdie?"

"Wait and find out," she said, hugging him tightly and kissing his wet cheek.

CHAPTER 31

Three weeks later, Birdie stared out a porthole at the coastline of Italy, wondering if it was all a dream. The last few weeks had been a whirlwind of activity, accepting a job with a cruise ship she didn't believe she'd even be in the running for, frantically scouring her bedroom for her never-used passport, then tediously deciding what she couldn't live without to take to her new 12X12 living space.

She hadn't told Hayden she was going until after she left, not wanting to make him think it was some kind of pathetic ultimatum. Only her parents, Sterling, and Duncan knew of her plans ahead of time. Not surprisingly, Sterling and her mother had been gung ho and excited for her. Duncan and her father had been equally morose and dire, upset over how her absence would affect them. Peas in a pod, those two.

You're going to get kidnapped, had been her father's dreary prediction.

You're going to fall in love with an Italian guy who will leave you high and dry, had been Duncan's.

Regardless, she kissed them each goodbye and sent a letter to Hayden, along with a key for his robot. She'd scoured everywhere to find one and then wrapped it with the message, "To wind yourself up. Your *you you* is too good to sit on the shelf."

She'd spent ten days training in London, trying not to gawk like the small-town Georgia girl she was, and now she was here, onboard, ready to start her new job. The ship sailed the Mediterranean, making stops in Italy, Greece, and Spain. The pay was exponentially more than she made working her last three jobs combined and, though the hours would be long onboard, she was also assured of enough down-time to eventually see all the same spots the tourists were paying great heaps of money to see. All in all, it was her dream. And if she felt a tiny bit of remorse for all she'd left behind, she told herself it was merely a bit of homesickness seeping through. After all, she would go the next twelve months without seeing a familiar face, a long time for a girl who had never been away from home before.

Her phone buzzed with a text from Hayden. She picked it up with a smile.

How is it?

I can see Italy from my window.

Amazing, isn't it?

YES! I can't believe I'm here.

I know, it's incredible. What do you think that big sticky uppy thing is, a lighthouse?

She peered closer, squinting. I think maybe it's a...wait, what?

. . .

SOMEONE TAPPED ON HER DOOR. "Come in," she called, voice wobbly. Surely he wasn't. Surely he didn't…

But he did, and he was. Hayden opened the door and leaned on the jamb. "Hey."

"Hay-den," she croaked, elongating his name into two broken syllables like Helen Keller discovering "water."

He came in and closed the door, sitting uninvited in the chair across from her desk.

"Wh-what are you doing here?"

"That's a long story. How much time have you got?"

She checked her watch. "Ten minutes."

He checked his watch. "What a coincidence. Me too." He grinned at her and extended his hand. "It's good to hear your voice. I'm Hayden Paxton, nice to finally meet you."

"Birdie Thompson, likewise," she said, confused as he enthusiastically pumped her hand. "Now can you tell me what's going on?"

"First can I say it's a real relief to hear another Georgia accent in these parts. I can't understand a dadgum word people are saying, even when they're speaking English. I asked someone for a Coke, and you know what they did? Gave me a Coke, didn't even check to see if I meant root beer or lemon lime or diet Pepsi."

"Hayden," she pressed.

"Right, right. I guess we're down to about eight minutes now. The thing is, Birdie, I thought I panicked when I saw Kaylee and Bryce at the funeral. I wrote you that letter with good intentions, wishing you well, practically sending you on your way. And then, you daft girl, you up and left me."

"You said…"

"I know what I said. Why would you ever listen? Clearly I'm a mess and in need of help. And *that* was when I panicked, when I realized you were good and truly gone. You want to know what it feels like to have your heart and lungs stop at the same time and refuse to function? I can tell you now for certain."

"But I can't go back. I'm committed to this job. I signed a contract for a year," she said.

"I know. I did, too," he said.

Her lashes fluttered. "What?"

"Well, see, I'm not the kind of guy who demands a woman give up her dream for him. I mean, this is an amazing opportunity. And I'm proud of you, by the way. Head of HR for an entire cruise ship. Wow. But it also turns out I'm not the kind of guy who can actually sit back and let the girl go. So what was I to do?"

"I honestly have no idea," she said. "Are you going to pay for every cruise as long as I'm employed?"

"Girl, no, I ain't made of money. Shoot, these people are so rich their sweat don't stink."

"Hayden," she pressed, growing impatient.

"Oh, right." He checked his watch again. "Four minutes."

"I know what I have in four minutes. What do you have in four minutes?"

"Work."

"What work?" she said.

He unzipped his jacket and showed her his uniform. "Turns out the ship had a last minute opening for a busboy."

"That is way beneath you," she exclaimed.

"It's all right. My girlfriend's the head of HR. I'm sure when something better comes along, she'll give me a leg up. In the meantime." He reached across the desk, plucked her out of her chair, and dragged her to him. "Hey."

"Hay-den," she returned, breathless now, heart fluttering.

"You have a nice voice, Birdie Thompson. You should use it more often."

"Someday when I won't shut up, you're really, really going to regret that statement," she said, easing her arms around him.

He nestled against her neck, sighing as if in relief. "I love you so."

"I love you more, but how are you magically okay now? It wasn't a month ago you were giving me the noble brushoff."

"The noble brushoff sounds like a line of toothbrushes for royalty.

And the truth is, I'm still not okay, far from it. I'm still grieving my lost marriage and my dad. but what I finally, blessedly realized is that I don't have to do that alone. I'm broken. You're broken. Let's pretty please be broken together 'cause I really don't think I can do it on my own. I love you, Birdie. I think I've loved you from that first minute, when you stepped in view of my door on your way to Sterling's shop, trying hard not to let your eyes look at me, talking to yourself out loud the whole time."

"You were the enemy," she explained.

"And now?" he prompted.

"And now you're the everything," she whispered, standing on her toes to kiss him.

He kissed her in return, the ship bobbing and lulling beneath them, the coast of Italy skimming in the background.

"I know you have to go, but I have one more question," he said, cupping her face lovingly in his palms, bestowing little kisses all over her cheeks.

"What?"

"What happens when two *you yous* get together?"

"I think we're a *we we* now."

He grinned. "Well, *we we*, all the way home."

"Forever," she said, and though it made her late for her first day inspecting the crew, and him too, she stood on her toes and kissed him again.

THANK you for reading *Blushing Birdie.* For more books, please check out my website at www.vanessagraybartal.com .